HER LITTLE SECRET

Women of Park Manor

ELLE WRIGHT

Her Little Secret
WOMEN OF PARK MANOR

Elle Wright

Rose Gold Press, LLC
Chicago, Illinois
www.RoseGoldPress.com
Editor:
Nicole Falls
Cover Design:
Sherelle Green

✻ Created with Vellum

Sex therapist, Paityn Young, couldn't get much sex in her city. So she developed her own line of naughty toys to get the job done. Now, she's bringing her talent to LA, hoping to launch her new company. Only her new business consultant has her thinking about more than just her product line.

As a favor to his boss, Bishop Lang agrees to help Paityn develop her new business. The only thing he knows about her is that she's off limits, but the moment he sees her, he realizes staying away might be harder than he thought. And his own personal journey may take a backseat to the blossoming relationship developing between them.

For my Lit Sisters, my Tribe! Thanks, Ladies, for making this journey that much sweeter.

Acknowledgments

God is awesome! I'm thankful to Him, first and foremost. I would be nothing without Him.

To my husband and children, thanks for supporting me through every low point, every success. I love you so much.

To my Rose Gold Press partners, let's do this! Love y'all!

To my sista friend, Sheryl Lister, you already know!

A special shout-out to the amazing readers and awesome writers that I've met on this journey. There would be no "Elle Wright" without your love and encouragement, your enthusiasm and understanding.

Dear Reader

Her Little Secret was such a labor of love!

I enjoyed delving into Bishop and Paityn, writing their forever. I loved getting to know the people around them. That Young family... Oooh wee! Just wait! They're coming.

I'm also elated that I got to work with my lit sisters on this series. Make sure you pick up the other books in the series. The Women of Park Manor are amazing! And so are the awesome authors who wrote them. It is an honor to write with these talented ladies. I'm grateful to call them sisters.

I hope you enjoy the ride!

Love,
Elle
www.ellewright.com

"Aw, he died?" Paityn stopped in front of a huge picture of the bellman, Buddy. The older man had been the first person she'd met at Park Manor, her new temporary residence. Buddy had immediately left an impression on her and she was sure he felt the same way about her.

"Damn," Paityn cursed when the bottom of her trusty duffle bag finally gave out spilling its contents on the sidewalk outside the luxury apartment community. She dropped to her knees and scooped several things into her arms.

"Miss, I can help you." The bellman hurried over to her with an empty box.

Mortified, Paityn struggled to hold onto her things but the long, plastic dick she'd hoped to keep hidden fell out of her arms and rolled toward the man. She felt heat rise up her neck to her ears as he picked up the plastic dildo, the prototype she'd molded herself.

Shrugging, he handed it to her. "Here, you take this, young lady. I'll take the other stuff."

"I'm so…" Embarrassed? Ashamed? Horny? Words escaped

her as she tried to figure out what she could say to make the entire situation more bearable.

The man grinned. "Don't worry. I always say, you got to do what you got to do. I'm Buddy." He shook her hand. "Nice to meet you."

"Paityn? Who died?"

She blinked, realizing she was still on the phone with her best friend, Rissa. "I'm… I have to go."

"Wait—"

"I'll call you back." She ended the call and approached the concierge, who stood near the entrance to Park Manor Bar & Tavern.

"Hi, Ms. Young," the portly man said. "Thank you for coming."

"I'm so sorry," she said. "He was always nice to me." Although she'd only been in the building for a few weeks, she'd talked to Buddy often. The last time they'd talked, he'd mentioned something about a vacation. When she hadn't seen him, she'd just assumed he was on someone's beach, not dead.

"I'm glad you could come and celebrate his life. Buddy was well-known in the building. We're expecting a large crowd, so we've assigned seats."

"Thank you," she told him.

Paityn hadn't really planned on attending a memorial that night. She'd planned on having shots and laughing with her best friend. Besides, she didn't know that man beyond polite talk and a few smiles. That's it. It wasn't like she could stand before the crowd and tell a story about his impact on her life. Talk of their first meeting would not be appropriate. Neither would the second time she'd seen him, the time a dick pic flashed across her cell phone screen just as he'd approached her in the lobby to let her know her Uber had arrived. For all she knew, he thought she was a nasty freak.

Maybe he wouldn't want her at his memorial. She'd never really sat down and talked to him about their awkward encounters. She'd never explained to the older man that it was her job to look at dicks. *Well, not really.* It was research. Because Paityn *wanted* to create the perfect dildo for her forthcoming line of naughty toys. And the picture was one of many that had been sent to her since she joined a popular dating website at her sister's request. It was a win-win. Her sister was in the process of creating a dating app for her matchmaking company and Paityn needed inspiration for her own business.

Buddy didn't know that, though. Buddy probably didn't care. Still, she couldn't *not* pay her respects. Even if she could only stay a short time.

As she approached the hostess, Paityn typed out a quick text letting Rissa know she'd be a little late to dinner. The hostess pointed her to a corner booth, where one woman was already seated.

After she introduced herself, she slid into the booth. Paityn had lived the majority of her life in Michigan, so she was happy to meet someone who'd lived in the area for a long time. Teegan owned Royal Essentials, a holistic store by the pier. She definitely planned to visit the shop in the near future.

A little while later, Kathi approached the table and shot her a sly grin—most likely at Paityn's expense. "I'm still laughing at your little incident," she said.

"Don't remind me," Paityn grumbled.

She'd met Kathi on her infamous first day at Park Manor, after the embarrassing incident with Buddy. Unfortunately, Paityn had done a terrible job at hiding her "toy" and her new neighbor had caught a glimpse of it in her box. It was the other woman's reaction and accompanying joke that had put Paityn at ease. The two had exchanged numbers right then and agreed to meet for dinner one evening.

The leasing manager, Burgundy, joined them next. Paityn was happy to see another familiar face at the table. Paityn's godfather, Jax Starks, owned the penthouse where she currently resided. And from the moment she'd arrived at Park Manor, Burgundy had been a godsend, ensuring her transition was seamless. As busy as she was, Burgundy always took the time to assist, whether that meant calling in a favor, recommending a restaurant, or helping Paityn get acclimated to the city. They'd worked out together at the Park Manor gym several times and she found Burgundy easy to talk to.

As usual, Paityn was met with wide eyes and open mouths when she told her tablemates about her day job. Paityn made her living as a sex therapist—one who hadn't had sex in a long ass time. That didn't change the fact that she was damn good at her job. She'd been published and even courted for reality television shows. More importantly, she'd helped many couples on their journey to good sex on the regular. Good sex was like fresh air. It relieved anxiety and cleared cluttered minds. It could warm you on a cold day. If only she could use all of her years of schooling and client experience to "get some" herself, she'd be all set.

It was unusual for Paityn to share much about herself with strangers. After all, she had seven siblings to talk to about any and everything. To her surprise, the conversation flowed easily, and Paityn quickly realized she had a lot in common with them.

Last to join their group was Skylar. Paityn had already had a thing for accents and smiled at her distinctive southern drawl. Sky looked like she had the weight of the world on her shoulders, though, and she wondered if it was because of Buddy. *Maybe they were really close?*

The dining room was crowded, standing room only, as people told stories about Buddy, laughed at jokes he'd told, and talked about the many ways he'd helped them. She appreciated the celebratory vibe of the memorial. No long eulogy, no stiff remarks, and no theatrics. Just good people celebrating a man's life. Paityn was grateful that she'd decided to attend. The memorial was a whole mood, in spite of the occasion, and it had given her a chance to connect with her new neighbors.

Aside from Rissa's family, she had nobody in the area. When Paityn packed up and moved to California, she'd wavered back and forth on her decision. Admittedly, she missed her life—*and family*—in Michigan.

Sure, her siblings annoyed her daily. They barged in on her at the wrong times to talk about their problems, gave unwanted opinions about her personal life, stole her clothes, and ate all of her food. But they were hers, and she'd never been so far away from them.

Talking, laughing, and drinking with the ladies reminded her of fun times with her sisters. For the first time since she'd moved, she felt a little less homesick. She felt like she'd made the right decision. Leaving her parents, her siblings, her friends, and her job behind to try and follow her dreams was huge for her, and Paityn felt empowered to go forth and embrace her new life choice.

Chapter 1

*I*f Paityn could ban two words, *fuck* and *shit* would be it. One made her think of toilets. The other? Well, let's just say she didn't need to be reminded of something she hadn't been blessed to do in years. And for the last ten minutes, she'd listened to her sister string those same two words together in varying combinations.

"Girl! Enough!" Paityn shouted, cutting her sister off mid-curse. "Road rage is really a thing. Get help." Pulling two sets of new sheets out of the dryer, she walked into one of the spare bedrooms and dropped the bedding on the mattress.

"Shit, I need to vent," Blake yelled. "It's your fuckin' fault I'm in this predicament. Michigan traffic doesn't make me want to kill someone."

Unable to help herself, Paityn giggled at her younger sister's antics. "You're a mess."

"Hey, I can only be me," Blake said.

The loud blare of the car horn followed by another colorful curse had her shaking her head in amusement. Some things would never change. Trump was still an asshole, she still couldn't eat beans to save her life, and Blake Young still had a potty mouth.

"I'm hanging up," Paityn told her sister. "I have stuff to do before you get here."

When "the brats" told her they were coming for a visit during the Memorial Day holiday, Paityn was ecstatic. Since her cross-country move, she'd seen her sisters countless times thanks to technology. But air kisses and virtual hugs didn't replace real face-to-face contact.

"Paityn?" Bliss called through the phone. She noted the rasp in her baby sister's voice, as if she'd been sleeping. "Are you making something for dinner? I'm hungry."

"Yes, ma'am." She walked the other set of sheets to the third bedroom and dumped them on the bed. "I'm making reservations. At this new Cuban restaurant Rissa told me about."

"Damn," Bliss muttered. "Will you at least cook breakfast in the morning?"

"You're so greedy," Blake said. "You just ate a whole foot-long sub and half of mine."

"I can't help it," Bliss shouted.

"I'm starting to think you're only here because you want me to cook for you." Paityn hurried to the kitchen and opened the oven. The homemade peach cobbler she'd prepared was almost done, Blake's favorite.

"No, I'm here because I miss you," Bliss said, just as Blake shouted another obscenity at a driver.

"That's good to hear." She also checked the macaroni and cheese baking in the bottom oven. *My favorite.*

"I wish Dallas could have come," Bliss mused. "I tried to get her to cancel her plans."

Paityn lifted the top off the pot on the stovetop, stirring the mustard and turnip greens a bit before she turned down the heat. "I do, too. But I'm not mad at her for taking a vacation out of the country. It's about time." She glanced at the Instant Pot on the countertop, noting the remaining time on the pulled pork, Bliss' favorite.

The truth? She did have reservations for dinner and dancing. Tomorrow. But, tonight, she also wanted to spoil her sisters a little. And it had been a while since she'd cooked anything of substance.

Growing up the second oldest child of a world-renowned couple, known for mending relationships and teaching others to parent, had a unique set of challenges. Partly because it was hard to live in her parents' shadows, but mostly because there were eight of them. Yes, Stewart and Victoria Young had eight damn children—willingly and happily. Paityn was the responsible sister, the oldest daughter, always offering a plate of food, a hand to hold, and a shoulder to cry on.

"Duke is pissed you didn't invite him," Bliss said.

Paityn laughed, thinking of the phone call she'd received from her brother earlier that morning. "I didn't invite y'all."

"But you're glad we're here," Blake added.

"I am, but I'm hanging up. I gave the concierge your names, so you should be able to come up without any problems. Don't kill anybody, Blake. See you soon."

Paityn ended the call after her sisters screamed good-bye. Shaking her head, she turned the dishwasher on and poured a glass of wine. When the oven timer went off, she pulled the dessert out and set it atop the island. The smell of peaches and cinnamon wafted to her nose and she resisted the urge to taste the cobbler.

She scanned the notes she'd jotted down earlier that day. The clitoral cream she'd hoped to perfect had been harder than she originally thought. Between her work as a sex therapist and her science background, it should have been a no brainer. Yet, she'd failed to even achieve the big "O" for the first two batches she'd made. Biting her thumbnail, she pondered her choice of ingredients. Maybe she'd used too much sodium benzoate?

Paityn scribbled an idea on the notepad and eyed the prototype she'd created. It was the fifth dildo she'd created and, by far, the best. She couldn't wait to show Blake and Bliss, which was why it was out in the open and not in her makeshift office-slash-lab.

Once Paityn had decided every woman needed a big ass dick, the wheels started spinning and a business idea formed. Paityn knew there were other sex aids on the market, entire stores dedicated to the business of pleasure, but she'd jumped in anyway. Now she was preparing to pitch her brand of sexual enhancement products.

When her stomach growled, Paityn glanced over at the peach cobbler. *One spoonful won't hurt.* She grabbed a wooden spoon and scooped a heaping helping out of the pan. Before she knew it one bite turned into two. Then, three. *Oh my God.* Four.

Fortunately, the knock on the door interrupted her greedy moment. She licked the spoon as she headed toward the door. She'd figured it would be at least thirty minutes before her sisters arrived. The airport was less than fifteen miles away, but it almost always took more than thirty minutes to get there in the infuriating 405 traffic.

She wiped a hand against her black leggings and opened the door. "You're her—"

Only it wasn't Blake or Bliss at the door. It wasn't even Rissa. No, the very *male* visitor standing there, his fist poised to knock again, was someone she didn't know. But damn, he was someone she probably *should* get to know.

Swallowing, she plastered a grin on her face and hoped

she looked presentable. "Hi." When he didn't answer immediately, she swallowed. *Maybe the hottie is a creeper?* But it wasn't like she was in some random apartment building. The concierge didn't just let anyone come up to the top floor.

The stranger's eyes dropped to her mouth and she absently wiped it with her sleeve, hoping she didn't have peach cobbler crust on her face.

"Can I help you?" she asked.

He blinked and then blessed her with the sexiest smile she'd ever seen up close. Pretty white teeth, adorably deep dimples, and beautiful creases framing full lips.

"I'm sorry. My name is Bishop." He held out a hand, presumably for her to shake it.

Her gaze dropped to it, noted his long fingers and clean fingernails, but she made no move to touch him. *Not yet.*

"I work at Pure Talent," he continued. "Jax Starks told me about you."

Paityn's eyes widened. "Oh, yeah. Bishop Lang."

Why is my voice so high? Probably because when her godfather told her he wanted her to meet one of the best legal minds on his team, she'd assumed it was an old, graying grandfather. A man that golfed on his off days and spent weekends at some highbrow country club drinking Burnt Martinis or scotch on the rocks. Not this fine ass man with smooth dark skin and a body that made her want to sing, "Do me, Baby". Because she was sure he'd be able to handle the job in a way no one ever had before. *Focus, Paityn.*

"Yes, that's me." His tongue darted out to wet his lips. "I live in the building and figured I'd come up and intro-duce myself."

Unable to turn away, she nodded. "Right. I think Uncle Jax did tell me that."

Briefly, she wondered if this was even a good idea, considering she couldn't stop staring at him. How would she be able to concentrate on business? But she trusted her godfather's judgment because he had never failed her and always had her best interests at heart.

From an early age, Paityn learned that blood didn't make family. And it was because of relationships like the one her father and Jax Starks had. The two men had grown up near each other in Detroit, Michigan and had even pledged the same fraternity. They were brothers in every sense of the word, even though they were born to different parents. Jax was her godfather, but he was also her "uncle".

She finally stepped aside. "Come in."

He followed her toward the kitchen. "Peach cobbler." The low groan that followed hit her right in the gut—or lower. "Smells good."

She gulped down the rest of her wine and dropped the wooden spoon into the sink. "I'm making dinner for my sisters." She turned the greens off and tried to recall everything her godfather had told her about Bishop. Clearly, she'd missed some things that he'd said. "I thought you were going to be out of town until next week?"

"I got back a little early."

Paityn leaned against the counter, meeting his intense gaze once again. "Cobbler?" she asked.

He looked down at the dessert and swallowed visibly. Nodding slowly, he said, "No."

Paityn frowned, surprised at his answer. Normally, a nod meant yes. "You sure? Because you look like you want some."

"I'm sure." He glanced at the pan again, before he looked up at her.

Tilting her head, she studied him. Something was preventing him from eating her cobbler. Did she want to know what? *Or who?* The need to know more welled up inside her. *It's the nature of my job to ask questions.* It wasn't his arms. Or the muscles stretching against the t-shirt he wore. The fact that he may be eating someone else's pie didn't bother her either. Well, not really.

Instead of probing further, she decided a change of subject was best. "Uncle Jax tells me you work in the business development department," she said. "But what else should I know?" Okay, so her attempt to sound professional came out more sultry than businesslike.

"What do mean?" he asked.

Clearing her throat, she added, "Because if we're going to work together, I'd like to learn a little more about your ass." Her eyes widened. "I mean, your experience?"

He chuckled. "I can give you the long version, or the short version."

Hello, sexual innuendo. She really did need to get some. Everything about this man and this interaction made her mind sink to the gutter. Paityn scratched her neck. "How about we start with where you're from?"

"Long Beach."

She opened the refrigerator and pulled out two bottles of water and offered him one. "Law school?"

"Berkeley." He took the water and twisted off the cap. "I've worked for the agency for fifteen years, and I've been instrumental in negotiating several business deals for agency clients. Jax has also entrusted me with many of his personal business matters."

"Good. What has he told you about me?"

His mouth curved into a smile. "He mentioned you were important to him and that I should take care of you."

She bit down on her lip. "I mean, about my business idea."

"Only that you were a sex therapist looking to start a new venture."

Paityn grinned, pleased that he didn't seem uncomfortable with her occupation like some men. "That's true. Did he tell you anything else?"

Bishop raised a brow. "No. I assume you will tell me the details."

"Right. I'll send you the draft of my proposal." She slid her notebook over and jotted down a note to herself. "I probably should have done this as soon as he gave me your email address, but I didn't want to interrupt your vacation. I know we always say we won't check emails on vacation, but we always do."

Ha barked out a laugh. "I don't disagree with that."

"Let me know when you're free to meet." She closed the notebook. "I have appointments during the day, but I'm usually free in the evenings." Paityn conducted her sessions online, via video chat or text therapy, which she'd found to be a great alternative to in-office therapy. Most of her clients loved the convenience and it allowed her to work from the comfort of her home, wherever that was.

"I'll check my calendar and get back to you. I have your numbers."

"Great. You'll have an email tonight. Not that I don't think you wouldn't read my proposal before we meet, but you definitely should. And preferably not in the office. In front of people."

The last thing she wanted was for a picture of her prototype to flash across his screen while he had someone in his office. That would be embarrassing, for him and for her.

Bishop frowned. "Why do I feel like I should be scared?"

Paityn laughed. "Because you should." She waggled her eyebrows.

"Now, I'm curious. Maybe you should give me a hint?"

"I would, but—" A knock on the door interrupted her explanation. "Excuse me. I have to get the door."

She ran to the door and opened it. Before she could say anything, Blake and Bliss surrounded her, hugging her tightly. Paityn wasn't overly emotional, but it felt good to hug her sisters, and she held on for longer than normal.

Finally pulling back, she smiled at the twins, noting the tears standing in Bliss' eyes. She brushed her cheek. "Don't cry."

"Please don't." Blake rolled her eyes. "It hasn't even been a month. Get it together."

"Leave me alone." Bliss elbowed Blake. "At least I don't have a black heart."

Paityn giggled. "Get in here." She pulled one of the rolling suitcases inside. "Are you hungry?"

Bliss patted her stomach. "You know it."

"I thought you weren't cooking," Blake said.

Paityn led them around the corner into the open living room area. "You know I wasn't going to let you come here without making your favorites."

"So, no Cuban food?" Blake asked. "Because I had my mouth set... Oooh wee. This place is gorgeous. Floor-to-ceiling windows, stunning artwork. And I love the color scheme. Everything just flows. Uncle Jax is doing big things."

Bishop glanced up from his phone and stood. "Hi."

Blake bit down on her thumbnail. "And apparently so are you," she muttered under her breath.

"Who is that, sissy?" Bliss whispered.

"And tell me he has a brother," Blake added.

Paityn rolled her eyes. "Shut up." She introduced them to Bishop. "He's an attorney at Pure Talent and he's helping me with my business."

"Oh, so you're helping her with the Big Ass D?" Blake asked, a wicked gleam in her eyes.

Bishop blinked. "Excuse me?"

Paityn glared at Blake. "He doesn't know about that yet," she said between clenched teeth. Leave it to her little sister to embarrass the hell out of her. "I'm sorry, Bishop. Don't mind her."

"Is that peach cobbler?" Blake asked.

"Yes," Bliss answered from the kitchen. She lifted the top off the pan. "And there's greens. And it smells like pulled pork. Yum."

Paityn shrugged when Bishop met her eyes. "Sisters."

"Right," he said. "I should probably get going, let you visit with your sisters. We'll talk."

"I'll walk you out."

He waved her off. "You don't have to."

"I do." Paityn walked him to the door. "Thanks for stopping by. I'm looking forward to working with you." She finally reached out to shake his hand.

When their palms met, she couldn't help but notice how the contact flooded her with warmth, from the tips of her fingers to her shoulders and throughout her body.

"It's good to meet you, Paityn." His husky, low voice made her want to lean into him.

She didn't, though. Slipping her hand from his, she nodded. "Right."

"I'll talk to you soon."

She nodded again. Because apparently she couldn't form any words.

Once he was safely outside the door, she exhaled. If every interaction with him ended with a handshake that somehow felt more like a kiss or a tender caress against her bare skin... *I'm definitely in trouble.*

Sighing, she padded back into the kitchen, where Blake was spooning a mound of cobbler into a bowl and Bliss was happily tasting the greens.

Blake glanced up at her, arching a brow. "You've been holding out, sissy. I need to know who Mr. Dark and Sexy is."

"I see you found the ice cream?" Paityn rounded the island and eyed the macaroni and cheese. Turning off the oven, she grabbed two potholders and pulled it out. She set it on the stovetop.

Bliss sniffed it. "You're the best."

Paityn shook her head. "You really are greedy."

"Can you imagine her pregnant and eating for two?" Blake asked.

"I don't even want to imagine," Paityn said, pulling the vinegar out of the cabinet and handing it to Bliss.

"Don't change the subject, Tyn." Blake scooped ice cream into her bowl. When the twins were small, they couldn't pronounce her name and had eventually settled on calling her a shortened version.

"What?" Paityn shrugged. "You saw him. He's fine. But he also works for Uncle Jax and he's going to help me with B.A.D." B.A.D. Toys was the proposed name of her company. "It would be irresponsible to mix business with pleasure."

"So," Blake said. "Irresponsible is fun. That's why it's irresponsible. And you definitely need some real dick. Not your prototypes." She shrugged. "Just sayin'."

"You get on my nerves," Paityn told her.

"She does have a point, Tyn," Bliss added. "You can't tell me that you weren't attracted to that man."

Paityn pointed at her greedy sister. "Not you, too. You're not supposed to agree with Blake."

"Hey, I just want you to be happy," Bliss said. "Have you met anyone on the sites you've been checking out for me?"

"If you count getting dick pics, fielding inappropriate comments, and blocking assholes, I'd say I've met a lot of people."

Paityn hadn't had a serious relationship since her divorce. In her defense, though, she hadn't really tried. And she wasn't sure she was ready to try. Work and family had taken up a lot of her time. Now, sex was a different story. For the first year, she hadn't minded the drought. Because she knew she needed the time to mourn the ten-year relationship. But now, two years later, it felt like a tragedy.

Blake snorted. "I know. I had to get off that damn site. They need to call it Plenty of Dicks because it's good for nothing else."

Laughing, Paityn stuck one serving spoon into the mac and cheese. "You ain't never lied. I might get off, too."

"I know, right?" Bliss agreed. "But you have to stay on because I need the intelligence for my app."

"Why can't you get on there?" Blake licked her spoon and groaned. "This shit is so good."

Bliss took a spoon and stole a bit of Blake's cobbler. "Because Tyler would not be happy with that."

When the Instant Pot timer went off, Paityn grabbed the coleslaw from the refrigerator. Then, she pulled three plates out of the cabinets and flatware from the drawer. "It's not like you're doing it for you. It's business."

Bliss made her living as a matchmaker. She enjoyed helping people find love and had recently decided to create an app to aid in her business. "Still, he doesn't want me looking at other men's parts."

"Tyler is a jerk." Blake took another bite of cobbler. "It's been past time to break up with his ass."

Bliss sighed. "He's not a jerk. And even if he was, he's my jerk."

"Seriously." Blake pointed her spoon at Bliss. "I counsel women—and some men—every day on how to break up with assholes and my sister is tethered to the biggest one of all."

Ironically, Bliss hooked people up and Blake was paid to help people break up. She earned a good living as a sort of breakup coach. People went to her when they needed help on severing unhealthy relationships.

"Paityn, tell her to shut up," Bliss grumbled. "I'm tired of her voice."

Shrugging, Paityn said, "I agree with her, Bliss. It's time."

"Anyway." Bliss tasted the macaroni. "This conversation was about you and Bishop."

"I don't understand why you two are so invested in this Bishop thing," Paityn said. "I just met him today."

"And you're attracted to him," Blake said, matter-of-factly.

"It's all in your face," Bliss agreed.

Blake met her gaze. "Ask him out."

"No." She shot her sister an incredulous gaze. "Besides, he didn't seem that interested." Even though Paityn recognized the flirt in him, she was sure he did that with every woman he encountered.

"Are you crazy?" Blake frowned. "You're single, you're fly, and you're not shy. So just do it."

"No," she repeated. Maybe a few years ago, she would have made the first move, but she couldn't imagine doing it now. She smacked a hand against the countertop. "Okay, I'm the oldest. Both of you shut the hell up and eat."

Yet, as her sisters fixed their plates, she couldn't help but think about Mr. Lang. Truthfully, she'd liked what she'd seen today. She sensed something deep in him, something more than his calm lawyerly demeanor suggested. And she couldn't help but find that even more intriguing.

Chapter 2

*G*ospel music, off-key singing, and the smell of fried food greeted Bishop when he entered his mother's house. It didn't matter what kind of day he had, he always felt peace wash over him when he stepped through the threshold of the Cameron Street home he'd grown up in.

Pictures lined the walls, the glass curio stood in the corner and the ceiling fan swirled slowly. It was home. Above the television hung a family picture. They were a family of four, two boys and loving parents. His nine-year old self sported a goofy smile as he stood in an awkward, forced pose. He remembered the day as if it were yesterday, the smell of the photography studio, the way his father had kissed his mother before they had to "say cheese". The pang that often accompanied thoughts of his father settled in. The aggressive cancer that claimed his father's life had tilted his world on its axis. Watching his hero struggle to walk or breathe or even speak had changed him in ways he never imagined. The realization that Bishop Deacon Lang

Sr. would never be able to enjoy retirement after working so hard and so long, still made him angry.

Bishop let out a heavy sigh. "Ma!"

"In the kitchen!" she shouted.

Bishop turned the television down and strolled into the kitchen, where Brenda Louise Lang stood over the stove, flipping chicken pieces with one hand and mimicking a choir director with the other hand. As usual, she also messed up the words to the song. She was still dressed in the pink scrubs she'd worn to work earlier, and her hair was pulled back into a ponytail. *Some things never change.*

Smiling, he approached her. "You still can't get the words right, huh?" He wrapped an arm around her and kissed her temple. "Hi, Ma."

"Don't do me like that, Junior." She grinned up at him and patted his cheek with her free hand. "My baby. I missed you so."

"Missed you, too." He studied her. Her bloodshot eyes confirmed what he'd suspected. She was tired. Despite his many pleas to retire, his mother had continued to work as a nurse practitioner at a local doctor's office. "When are you going to leave that job?"

"When I feel like it." She forked the last few pieces of chicken out of the frying pan and onto a plate. Once she turned off the stove, she turned to him and pulled him into a warm embrace.

There was something about a hug from his mother that made everything wrong in his world right. And Bishop soaked it all in. It had been a long time since he'd seen his mama, and he was happy to be in her presence again.

Finally, she pulled back. "Are you hungry? I made most of your favorites. Couldn't get to the store to get the pie crust for peach cobbler, though. I'll fix it for you Monday."

Bishop's mind wandered to the peach cobbler he'd

turned down earlier, and the woman who'd made it. Paityn Young had been a surprise to him from the moment she'd opened her door, wooden spoon in hand. He didn't know what he'd expected, but he didn't expect *her*.

Working for Pure Talent for as long as he had, he'd heard about Paityn. He'd even been around her family on numerous occasions, partied with her brother Duke. Despite his lack of interest in social media, he was sure he'd seen pictures of her on someone's profile. *Maybe Instagram?* But he'd never met her. They'd never locked eyes in person. Not at a party, not at work, or even at Xavier Starks' house. Because if he had, he would have remembered the soft rasp of her voice, that dimple on her right cheek, those full hips, and the way her eyes seemed to see everything. *Working with her might be a problem.* Especially if he couldn't stop staring at her. Or flirting with her. And he'd done so shamelessly and deliberately.

Turning down her offer for dessert had been necessary for their working relationship. It was already weird enough that he was drawn to her from the moment their gazes locked, curious about her in a way that felt foreign to him because it had been so long. They'd just met, yet somehow he felt that eating with her would be a lot more than just food.

And Bishop didn't eat anyone else's cobbler because no one made it better than the woman standing next to him humming softly to the music. Still, the sweet smell of peaches, cinnamon, and dough made him want to break his rule, if only for a small taste. It did look good. Hell, *she* looked good. And if her peach cobbler was better than his mother's, he'd be in trouble for real.

"Baby, are you okay?"

He blinked, shaking thoughts of Paityn Young from his mind to focus on his favorite girl. "I'm good. Gabe coming through?" His brother had texted him earlier to let him know he might not make it to dinner.

His mother shrugged. "If he can get away from the hospital on time. I told him to bring the girls, but he said they had a birthday party."

Bishop was a proud uncle to two beautiful, intelligent nieces—Hayley and Hayden. And they had him wrapped around their fingers. "They'll be here on the holiday, though."

Every Memorial Day, his mother barbecued and invited the entire Lang family over. Too much food, alcohol, dominoes, and shit talking. All day. It was a tradition he'd always looked forward to.

"Did you want me to bring anything?" he asked, picking up the plate of chicken and taking it to the kitchen table. He took a seat. "I can bring drinks or something. Ice."

She giggled. "There you go. With your non-cooking self." Ma set the buttery mashed potatoes and green beans on the table. "You can come help me with the grill."

Groaning, he said, "Fine. I'll be here."

Soon, she joined him, plopping down in her chair with a heavy sigh. As they ate, they made small talk about family, the church gossip she always seemed to know about, and his job.

"How was your trip?" She pointed at his plate. "You better eat that chicken, boy."

He chuckled. "You know I'm trying to eat better, ma. I keep trying to tell you to bake the chicken. Too much fried food is not good for you."

She waved a hand over his plate. "Oh hush, one piece won't hurt. You're getting too skinny anyway."

Bishop had recently lost thirty pounds, mostly because he'd stopped drinking beer every day. Clean eating had been one of the many changes he'd made over the past two years.

He bit into a drumstick. "Better?"

His mother smiled. "Much." She sighed. "I worry about you."

"I'm fine."

She placed a hand over his. "Are you sure? After Roderick died, I wasn't sure you'd be okay."

Bishop didn't want to talk about his best friend. He didn't want to think about the loss he'd suffered within the past few years. Because he'd barely emerged from the crushing grief that had consumed him after his father died when he'd heard the news of his friend's death. To think of Rod dying alone, collapsing during a run still made him sick. They'd been more like brothers than friends. From the Hilltop Home Daycare to the night before Rod took his last breath, they'd had each other's back through everything from broken hearts to broken vows.

Roderick didn't have any family. Bishop shared *his* mother and brother with Rod. Yet, that fateful morning, Bishop wasn't there for his friend. Instead of meeting him like he normally did on Saturdays, he'd been distracted with work.

"Son, maybe you should talk to someone," his mother suggested.

He shook his head. "I don't need to talk to anyone, Ma. I'm fine."

"I just don't want you to…" She trailed off, but he knew what she was thinking.

"End up like Rod?" he finished.

She dropped her gaze, smoothed a shaky hand over the tablecloth. His mother raised them in the church, instilled a life of faith and obedience to the Most High. When they weren't at school, they were at church; and it was that way until he graduated from high school and went away to college. Every day, his mother told him about grace and mercy, warned him to "get his life right." Not that he lived a fast life. Unlike Rod, he didn't fill his nights with meaningless women and booze. He worked hard. For years, it seemed that was all he did.

"I loved Rod, but I don't want you to end up like him. That would be a shame."

He closed his eyes, took in a deep breath. "Ma, please. Stop. I know you're concerned, but you don't have to worry about me. I am good. That's why I went away."

Bishop had needed to re-center himself. So, he'd taken the time to be alone, to meditate, to pray. He started with his body, removing processed foods from his diet, limiting his alcohol intake, and working out more than twice a week. He spent less time thinking about contracts and more time focusing on his spirit.

"I'm going to take your word for it," his mom said. "I'm glad you took the time off. You needed to be away from work."

He snickered. "Look who's talking. You don't have to work. The house is paid off. Me and Gabe are here for you. You can come stay with either one of us. Or we can get you a condo somewhere you don't have to worry about the lawn or crazy neighbors."

She rolled her eyes. "I love my house. Me and your father worked hard to pay it off."

His parents had set an example for him and his brother. Gabe graduated from medical school and worked as an orthopedic surgeon. And Bishop had never wavered from his career track. He'd climbed the ladder at Pure Talent and loved the work he did for the agency.

"I love my independence," she continued. "I need to work. It keeps me busy so that I'm not sitting here alone, missing your father. But trust me, I know when to sit my ass down."

Bishop barked out a laugh. It was rare but hearing his mother curse always amused him. He lifted his arms in surrender. "Okay, okay. Don't pull out the big guns and start cussing me out, Ma."

"Not even here twenty-four hours and you already got Ma cussing?" Gabe walked into the living room.

Bishop stood, pounding fists with his little brother before embracing him. "What's up, bruh?" Gabe leaned down and kissed their mother's brow. "Hi, Ma. I told you about that fried chicken."

She shoved Gabe playfully. "Boy, stop."

Gabe washed his hands and sat down next to Ma. "I'm just playin' with you. I'll happily eat it." He transferred three wings onto his plate. "What are y'all talking about?"

"Nothing," Bishop said. "Ma was just being Ma. Telling me to do something she's not willing to do herself."

"This conversation is not supposed to be about me. When I have you two over for dinner, I want to hear about your lives. Like for instance, Gabe and Cynthia aren't having more kids."

"Hell no," Gabe murmured.

Ma smacked his brother's shoulder. "Watch your mouth."

Gabe rolled his eyes and bit into a piece of chicken. "Sorry, Ma."

"As I was saying. Junior, you need to find you a nice young woman to give me more grandchildren."

Bishop choked on his sweet tea. "Yeah, we're not having this discussion either."

"What? Sister Jones' granddaughter is lovely. And single. You should come to Family and Friends Day at the church to meet her."

ELLE WRIGHT

Gabe laughed. Bishop glared at him. *Hell. No.* He cringed when he thought of the last time he visited his mother's church. The way those old women tried to pawn off their daughters and granddaughters, and the occasional pinch on the ass, had done him in for the day.

Ma frowned. "What's so funny, Gabe?"

"Nothing." His brother shrugged. "Sister Jones' granddaughter is a gem. You'd especially love that bland pound cake she brings to the church picnic every year."

Bishop covered his mouth to hide his smile. Because he'd had that pound cake and had to drink two bottles of water when he almost choked on it.

"What's wrong with you? You're happy with Cynthia, and you met her at church."

Unlike Bishop, Gabe attended Sunday service most weeks. But he suspected that had a lot to do with the fact that he'd married the pastor's daughter.

"That's not true, Ma," Bishop said. "He met her at school and knew that he had to go to church to get close to her."

"Still," she argued. "Lily Jones is a beautiful girl."

"That's not going to happen, Ma." Bishop kissed her hand. "Love you, though."

"You need a wife," she insisted.

"I need a nap," he countered.

"Junior!" She swatted him with a napkin. "Stop playing with me."

"Ma, I don't need you to hook me up with Sister Anybody's kid."

"Are you dating?"

He shrugged. "I don't know. Sometimes."

"Are you getting busy?"

"Whoa!" Bishop and Gabe exclaimed simultaneously.

Bishop stood. "Those words should never come out of

28

your mouth." Because talking about sex with his mother was not what's up.

"I agree with that," Gabe said.

"You've always been too particular when it comes to women," she babbled on. "Remember that stuck up thang you brought over here a few years ago? She didn't even want to drink out of my glasses. Like I keep a dirty house. I wanted to bop her upside the head."

Once again, Gabe cracked up at his expense. "That was crazy."

Bishop remembered that night vividly. Between Clarice turning her nose up at everything his mother served, and the way Ma clenched her fork like she wanted to stab his girlfriend, he'd vowed never to bring another woman home unless he was ready to make her Mrs. Lang.

At forty, he'd thought about what it would mean for him to settle down. In the past, he'd been with women who only cared about his money or his status. He didn't care for the games some women played. *Chase me, romance me, spoil me.* The sound of Clarice's high-pitched, whiny voice replayed in his mind. That's all he'd heard from sunup to sundown with Clarice, until he got tired of their relationship being all about her and what she wanted.

Ma stood. She tilted her head, assessing him with eyes clouded with tears. She gripped his chin in her hand, like she'd done for as long as he could remember. It was a comforting gesture, one that made everything better—even if for a short time. "I'm so proud of you. And I love you so much. I just want the best for you, son. You've lost so much. I want to see the light back in your eyes."

"I love you, too. I'll be okay."

"You will. Once you get a wife." She grinned. "Just kidding. Take your time. But not too much time, because I want to be able to play with my future grandkids. Or take a walk with them without the aid of a cane."

Gabe snickered, while he continued to eat like it was the first and last time he would ever have their mother's fried chicken.

Bishop shook his head. "You're hilarious, Ma."

"I know. You always tell me that." Her phone buzzed and she picked it up, squinting at the screen. "Let me get this. It's Sister Lou. She probably wants to tell me about choir rehearsal." Ma answered the phone and disappeared down the hall.

Pushing his plate away, Gabe asked, "How was the vacation, bruh?"

Bishop tapped the table. He'd spent the first few weeks in South Africa, before traveling to Israel and then Dubai. "Much needed."

"How are you?"

Leaning forward, Bishop clasped his hands together. "I'm good, bruh. Like I told, Ma, I'll be alright."

"Rod was important to all of us, and I hate that he died the way he did."

Bishop nodded. "Yeah. While I was away, a distant cousin contacted me about his house."

Gabe shook his head, disgust twisting his mouth. "What the hell? As long as we've known Rod, he never mentioned any relatives. And now they're coming out of the woodwork."

"Exactly." It was a shame. Since Rod died, Bishop had been contacted by "supposed" family members and even women claiming to have had his friend's children. Most messages, he'd deleted. Others, he'd responded in a not-so-nice way.

Gabe leaned back, crossed his legs at the ankle. "What are you going to do with his place?"

Rod had purchased a loft near Park Manor before he died. And since Bishop held power of attorney, he was responsible for the estate. "Sell it. I've already been in touch with a realtor. I plan to go in and clean out his stuff."

"If you need help, I'm here."

Bishop appreciated the offer. "I'll let you know."

His brother squeezed his shoulder. "Now how did you and Ma end up talking about Sister Jones and her grand-daughter?"

Chuckling, Bishop said, "Ma is trippin'."

"Definitely. But listen…" Gabe sighed. "Cynthia has a friend at work that she wants you to meet."

"What? Not you, too."

"I just told her I'd bring it up. Now, I don't have to lie and say I did."

"Tell your wife——"

"Your sister-in-love," his brother added.

"My sister," Bishop corrected. He'd known Cynthia since they were kids. She was more than an in-law. "Tell her that I don't need help."

"I got you."

"We all need a little help," Ma said, strolling back into the kitchen. Instead of stopping at the table, she went straight to the sink and proceeded to wash the dishes. "It's funny. Sister Jones just asked about you."

"I have to go, Ma." Bishop stood.

She turned. "Okay, okay. I'm done. Promise me one thing, though."

Raising a brow, he said, "Not until you tell me what I'm promising." He'd learned that lesson the hard way, when he'd ended up escorting the pastor's daughter to a cotillion in high school.

"Just don't bring another Clarice home. I can't take it."

Laughing, he assured her, "You don't have to worry about that."

Bishop didn't make the same mistake twice. He didn't want to jump back into a similar situation. For now, he was centered, he was healthy, he was content. And until he met someone that made him want to rethink that position, he was good.

Chapter 3

"*I* figured it out." Paityn sipped on her sangria. The crowd at La Vida Havana Cuban Lounge was lit. The food was delicious, and the live band encouraged dancers of all experience levels to hit the floor.

Rissa swayed in her seat to the beat. "What are you talking about?"

"She doesn't know," Blake added, taking a shot of tequila.

They'd been at the restaurant for a couple of hours, eating, laughing, and drinking. It felt good to be out and about with some of her faves. "I do. I've been thinking about this all day." *And all night.* "I think the reason I thought Bishop was so sexy and hot and beautiful was because I'm horny. He's probably not even that fine in real life."

Frowning, Blake popped a green olive into her mouth and chewed slowly, almost like she was trying to analyze what Paityn had just said. "Hm. No, he really is that fine."

"Seriously fine," Bliss added with a decisive nod. "You didn't imagine that, Tyn."

Paityn threw her hands up in surrender. "Whatever."

"Bishop?" Rissa narrowed her eyes. "Bishop Lang?"

Paityn's mouth fell open. "You know him?"

Her best friend grinned. "Yes! And he is… Oooh wee. I don't know many women who wouldn't think he was fuck-withable."

"Girl!" Blake gave Rissa a high five.

"Seriously," Rissa continued. "Bishop is a good friend of Rick's."

Paityn smiled at her friend. Rissa had been dating Rick for years and still lit up when she talked about him. "That's cool."

"They're actually shooting pool tonight. I don't even know why I didn't put two and two together. Bishop works for Pure Talent. I should have known Jax would have him assist you with the B.A.D." Rissa leaned forward, lowering her voice. "Speaking of, does Bishop know what you're trying to do?"

"He will when he reads the proposal I sent him last night." Paityn had stayed up late reviewing her documents, correcting graphics, and fact-checking statistics. And it had taken an hour for her to actually send it once it was done because she wanted to let it sit for a bit in case she wanted to change something. "He confirmed receipt, so…" She shrugged. "We'll see."

"We told her she should ask him out," Bliss shimmied her shoulders to the beat.

Rissa squealed. "That's perfect. I had thought about trying to hook him up with Zara, but I don't think they'd mesh well together."

Paityn found it interesting that Rissa had considered a match between Bishop and her younger sister. Zara Reid was a sports agent, worked in a similar industry. She would think Zara had more in common with Bishop than she did.

And if she asked for more details, Rissa would take that as permission to run with it.

"Want me to talk to him?" Rissa asked.

"No!" Paityn and Bliss said simultaneously, before they broke out into a fit of laughter.

Paityn loved her best friend, but Rissa was too forward and tended to share too much due to the fact that she had no filter. She patted Rissa's hand. "I'm good, hon. I'm not going to ask him out."

"What?" Blake shot her an incredulous stare. "Why the hell not? We've already been through this."

That part was true. Last night, they wouldn't let the subject drop. Not during dinner, the Netflix chick flick marathon, or breakfast that morning. "You've been through this. And you know me. When do I listen to you and Bliss? You're in a different age group."

Blake waved a dismissive hand toward her. "Whatever. You're not that much older than us."

"No, I get what she's saying," Bliss said. "She's had an entire set of experiences that we haven't had. Being a married woman, then a divorced woman are two distinctive lifestyles."

"Exactly," Paityn agreed.

"In light of that, I think your soulmate is somewhere unhappily married to an ungrateful woman," Bliss announced. "Give him time to free himself from that and he'll find you."

"Really, Bliss?" Paityn asked. "Why would I want some damaged wimp who can't stand up for himself and leave an unhealthy relationship? Then, I'll be the unhappy woman married to the needy man!"

"Paityn, what happened to you?" Blake finished her drink and ordered another. "Bliss is the dramatic one. Not you."

"Hey!" Bliss said.

"Well, shit, I'm almost fifty!" Paityn shouted. "I need my future booty call and potential soulmate to hurry up and figure his shit out so we can get this party started."

Blake rolled her eyes. "You're not even forty! What the hell?!" The waiter with the tight ass and sexy smile chose that moment to reappear. Blake winked at him and pointed at Paityn. "Get her a drink. And not one of those fruity joints you've been serving all night. She needs something that will put some hair on her chest. I can't have two needy sisters." She slammed her fist down on the table. "Man up, sis."

They dissolved into a fit of laughter.

Wiping tears of mirth from her eyes, Paityn said, "I love y'all. Thanks for coming to see me."

"She might be a little drunk," Rissa muttered.

"I'm not!" Paityn scanned the room. Since they'd arrived, many men had approached their table and asked them to dance, but she hadn't felt like getting up. "I just don't know what's wrong with me. Look at him." She pointed at the man that had been standing at the bar watching them for the past twenty minutes. "He looks like a creep. It's not 1975. Why is he flashing a chest full of hair? I'm convinced I missed my guy wasting so much time with Philip."

Blake grunted. "I told you to break up with his ass five years before you actually did."

Bliss elbowed Blake. "Shut up. Don't listen to her, Paityn."

Rissa squeezed her knee. "You were married, committed. You gave it your all. That's all you *can* do in any given situation."

In her attempt to "make her marriage work", she'd lost herself. Despite everything that she told her sisters and her clients, she'd let him manipulate her from day one. She'd accepted his lies, his excuses. He'd given her years of grief, nothing but uncertainty. And she'd stayed with him too long.

It had taken her a while to even look at another man, to even want to share her bed with anyone else. Now that she'd opened herself up to the possibility of a new situation, she felt scared. Vulnerable.

"You're right, Blake," Paityn conceded. "I knew all of the signs and still stayed. Which is why I'm hesitant to start something here. Who knows how long I'll stay? I can work from anywhere. I like LA, but I miss my house, my bed. Why start a relationship when—?"

"Let me stop you there." Blake sliced the air with her hand. "Who said anything about a relationship? I thought we were talking about sex."

"Blake, you're… I don't want to talk about this anymore." Paityn folded her arms across her chest. "I'm not twenty-five. I don't just have sex for the hell of it." Even though, she kind of wanted to.

"Why not? That shit is fun." Blake slid closer to her. "Okay, I'm a bitch. I probably *don't* get it, because I'm not you. I haven't lived your life. But you're my big sister, and I hate to see you like this."

Paityn scanned their faces, noted the concern in their eyes. Tears welled up in her eyes. *This is some BS.* Crying in the middle of salsa night?

"Don't mess up your makeup, sis." Blake dabbed a napkin under Paityn's right eye, then her left. "You're too hot for raccoon eyes."

She laughed. "You're crazy."

"Maybe. But I love you. And I'm going to need you to stop boxing yourself in? There's no good reason for you not to follow your body's cues. Isn't that what you've always told me?"

Bliss nodded. "That sounds just like her."

"You're attracted to him. Why aren't you letting yourself feel it? Tyn, you're already skipping ahead to a future no one can be sure of. Why plan the breakup before the hookup? Concentrate on the now."

Rissa waved a napkin in the air. "That's a word right there"

Paityn stuck her tongue out at her bestie. "You're right." She sighed. "I do need to stop overthinking things and focus on now."

"Yes." Blake smirked. "And right now, Bishop is looking fine as ever in those dark jeans and that white button-down shirt."

Paityn blinked. "Huh?"

Blake turned Paityn's head toward the door, where Bishop and Rick stood scanning the crowd. "And if you don't step to him, I will," her sister muttered. "Because… damn."

Paityn's eyes flashed to Rissa just in time to see the wicked smile form on her friend's lips. "Did you call Rick?"

Shrugging, Rissa said, "I just texted him and told him where we were. And I mentioned I might be a little too drunk to drive home."

"You are so…?"

"Slick?" Bliss said.

Blake finished her drink. "More like brilliant."

When Rick spotted them, he pointed and the two men started toward their table. Paityn took a moment to catalogue Bishop as they neared the table. He definitely knew how to wear an outfit—not too big, not too small. *Perfect fit.* His skin seemed to glow in the dim lighting. And his walk… It rivaled King T'Challa's. Blake had called it right. *Damn*.

Bishop's gaze met hers when they stopped in front of them. He smiled. And she? Giggled like a freakin' damn teenager. What. In. The. Hell. It was the alcohol. *That's my story and I'm sticking with it.*

Rick smiled. "What's up, ladies?" He kissed Rissa. "Are you okay?"

"I'm fine." Rissa grinned up at her man. "I just didn't want to drive myself home. Too much sangria." Her friend waved at Bishop. "Hey. Sorry to interrupt your night."

"You're good," Bishop greeted them. "Good to see you again." Once again, his gaze landed on her, raked over her. There was no mistaking the heat blazing in his dark eyes.

Paityn couldn't look away if she tried. Blake's words swirled around in her head. *Concentrate on now.*

Blake stood and pulled Bliss to her feet. "It's time for us to go somewhere else."

Paityn chuckled. Leave it to her sister to shoot it straight at all times. She got that from their father. "Okay."

Her sisters disappeared into the crowd, and soon Bishop was seated next to her. Rissa and Rick were still there, and she knew her friend was watching them like a hawk. But she couldn't care.

"Small world," she said. "I had no idea you knew Rick."

The corner of his mouth quirked up. "We went to Berkeley together."

Bishop explained that he'd met Rick while pledging the same fraternity. They'd also attended law school together. "It seems we're connected in ways that make it seem extremely unbelievable that we've never met before. I know your parents. I've actually hung out with your brother, Duke."

"Now, that doesn't surprise me. Especially if you're cool with X." Xavier Starks also worked for Pure Talent. Her brother and X were like brothers. "I don't think there are many people who know X that don't know Duke. And my parents…" She shrugged. "They're well known. And clients of the agency."

The waiter came over to the table. "Can I buy you a drink?" he asked her.

And he has manners. "Sure. I'll have another sangria." Bishop ordered her drink, but only ordered himself a bottle of water. "You're not going to have a drink with me?"

He shook his head, running a hand over his trimmed beard. "Nah, I'm good."

She observed him. "I can't figure you out, Bishop Lang."

Raising a brow, he asked, "Do you want to?"

"Maybe."

That low, husky chuckle that always seemed to catch her off guard once again did its job and she crossed her legs. Tightly. To quell the sudden ache that had settled into her core. There was no question about it. She definitely wanted him. But she wasn't about to play her cards so fast and loose.

Paityn hadn't missed the curious stares of many of the women in the restaurant. He probably attracted attention everywhere he went. He just had that aura about him. Which meant she needed to tread lightly.

She glanced over and was surprised that Rissa and Rick weren't next to them. *When did they leave?* She craned her head around, trying to find her friend and her sisters. Paityn spotted Bliss on the dance floor and Blake at the bar. But no Rissa.

"They disappeared around the back," Bishop offered. "I think she had to go to the restroom."

"Ah. Thanks." She shifted in her seat, turning to face him. "Did you read my proposal yet?"

He laughed softly. "I did. And I have two questions."

"What?"

"Does Jax know the specifics about this business idea?"

Paityn threw her head back in laughter. "He does. Why?"

"I can't imagine that conversation."

"Trust me, it was hard. But at the same time, it wasn't. I don't know how to explain it. Uncle Jax has always had an open-door policy. He's supported everything I've ever wanted to do. Just like my parents."

He leaned into her, shoulder to shoulder. Like they'd been doing that for years. It was so natural, comfortable. "Still, I would have loved to see his reaction."

She beamed, thinking about that particular meeting. She'd flown into Atlanta for a conference. While there, she'd visited the Pure Talent office to have lunch with Uncle Jax. Giggling, she told Bishop the story about how Uncle Jax nearly spilled his sweet tea all over his expensive suit when she showed him her prototype. But once he'd recovered, he'd given her invaluable advice.

"And now, I'm here." She thanked the waiter, who'd arrived with her drink.

"You seem pretty close with Jax."

"I am. All of us are."

When her father took a teaching position at UCLA, he'd rented a home in the Brentwood neighborhood where Jax and his family resided. She counted that period as one of the best times of her life. It was there that she'd met Rissa, who had lived next door to Uncle Jax.

Paityn didn't know a world without the Starks family. She had fond memories of Christmas parties, New Year's Eve excursions, and exotic vacations with her extended family. When she told her uncle about her plans, he'd offered his penthouse without reservation or hesitation, and immediately made calls to associates that he felt could help her.

"What about you?" she asked, taking a sip of her drink. "Are you and my uncle friends or do you just work for him?"

Bishop hunched a shoulder. "I'd say he's an uncle-like figure in my life. He took me under his wing when I started working at the agency, helped me rise up the ranks quickly. I appreciate him."

She nibbled on her bottom lip, and he followed the movement. "He's good like that." They talked for a few moments about his work at the agency and her client work. Finally, she asked, "You said you had two questions. What was your other question?"

He blinked. "Oh, yeah. I did want to know something else."

"Shoot."

"Why this?"

"I'm not sure what you mean."

"Why this business?"

"Well," she sighed, "Because women don't just need a dick to have an orgasm."

————

Bishop stared at the woman who'd captivated him from the moment he'd walked into the Cuban restaurant that evening. Paityn was so refreshing, albeit confusing. One moment she was flustered and the next she was a boss.

When Rick cut their game of pool short to come to

Rissa's rescue, he hadn't expected to end up face-to-face with the beautiful Paityn. The black jumpsuit she donned had a plunging neckline and a lace top. She was fully covered, classy and classic, and the sexiest woman in the lounge. Her brown skin shimmered like a beacon of light on a foggy night. Yesterday, her hair had been straight. Tonight, her short hair was full of soft waves that he wanted to run his fingers through.

To top it off, she'd spoken to him like she didn't care what he thought of her. Which made him even more interested to hear what she had to say.

Leaning in, he whispered, "Care to explain?"

Admittedly, he'd been floored when he skimmed the proposal that morning. Bishop rarely felt taken aback by anything, but reading her words had definitely knocked him off his square initially. But as he'd studied the particulars, he found himself wondering a few things about her. What made her want to delve into that particular business? Did her boyfriend not know how to satisfy her? Did she even have a man? Did Paityn test the products on herself? *Would she let me watch?*

Bishop shook his mind clear of those thoughts because it wouldn't get him anywhere. The attraction was obvious *and* mutual. But there were several reasons why he shouldn't go there. First and foremost, she was Jax's goddaughter and his boss trusted him to help her get her business up and running. He didn't want to jeopardize years of respect.

She beamed. "Definitely. I've heard so many stories from women through the years. Did you know that approximately eighty percent of women have never had an orgasm through intercourse?"

He didn't know that. He answered with a quick shake of his head.

"And that doesn't even include the women who have never come at all," she continued. "I concluded that a big reason for that is because many women don't know their own bodies. So many have never even looked at their lady bits up close."

"Why do think that is?"

Paityn set her glass down on the table. "A variety of reasons. Religion, upbringing... It varies. Some churches teach that masturbation is a sin. And I'm here to tell them it's okay, and even healthy to know what your body needs in order to climax. So, I figured why not throw my hat into the sexual enhancement ring. I wanted to create something for women who wanted that big O. Single women, like me, who haven't found someone worth her body and her mind. Or women who are on a spiritual journey and just need a release. Or maybe someone has a man who just can't get her there. And I want to help them. I want to make it okay for women—black women—to get theirs."

The way her eyes lit up when she talked about her work made him want to carve out hours to explore her. He'd also spent an inappropriate amount of time watching her mouth, telling himself that it wouldn't be a good idea to run his fingers over the bottom lip she loved to nibble on. Her scent drove him crazy. She smelled like fruit and flowers, like freedom and fun. And he was rock hard. In the middle of the damn restaurant, while people were dancing and eating, while she was rambling on about sex and orgasms like she had no clue how she affected him.

She laughed softly, shifted in such a way that her arm brushed up against his. He bit back a groan at the contact. "You probably didn't want to hear all of that," she said. "But that's the shortened answer to your question."

Bishop leaned back, tried to play it cool when all he really wanted to do was perch her on his lap and let her demonstrate her techniques. "Interesting," he managed to say.

"I think so," she said. "But enough about me. I have a question for you."

Arching a brow, he asked, "Should I brace myself for this?"

Her mouth curved into another smile. This time, the beauty mark above her upper lip commanded his attention. "Are you single?"

"Are you asking for a friend?"

"No." She laughed. "You're funny, though."

Bishop would never categorize himself on the funny spectrum. That was always Gabe or Rod. Most women he knew would consider him serious. To hear Paityn call him funny did something to him, made him want to invest in making her laugh.

"You think so?" he asked.

She leaned back; eyes narrowed. "Why? Don't you?"

Shrugging, he shook his head. "Not really."

"Well," she placed her hand on his hand, "You're funny to me. And that's really all that matters, right?"

"Right."

"So?"

He forced his attention away from her hand on top of his to her face. "So, what?"

"Are you single?"

He sighed. "Yes. But I hope you don't think I'm ready be hooked up with your 'nice' friend."

Paityn giggled. "I definitely don't think that." She sighed. "Obviously, you're attractive."

"Am I?"

She shoved him playfully. "I'm trying to be serious, and maybe a little flirty. And just so you know, if I was thinking of a hookup, it would be for myself."

Damn. The woman in front of him was fearless. Or at least, she wanted him to think she was. It must have been the setting, the Latin music, the lighting, the drinks he hadn't consumed but felt like he did. Because he didn't care if she was his boss' goddaughter. He didn't care about anything at that moment. Only her—him and her, her on top, her beneath him, him behind her

"But I don't know," she said. "You might be a player."

He laughed. "Why would you think I'm a player?"

Shrugging, she motioned toward the bar. "I'm sure you've noticed the women over there trying to get your attention. They're not subtle."

He didn't make a move to look toward the bar. Yes, he'd seen them. He wasn't interested. "If I were a player—"

"Oh Lord," she grumbled, with an eye roll.

"Which I'm not," he continued. "Would that change this conversation a little?"

"A lot," she admitted.

"Okay." He met her gaze. "There are many reasons why I'm not a player. One, my vibe is too dope to be just giving my energy to anybody." He leaned in, so close he could feel her sweet breath on his lips. "And two, I don't like games."

Paityn let out a slow, shaky breath. "Oh. Well, in that case, I—"

"I'm sorry. I'm so sorry. Tyn?"

Paityn jumped away from him and nearly fell out of her chair. "Blake!"

Her sister stood in front of them, her hands together like she was praying Paityn wouldn't hurt her for inter-rupting.

"I hate to do this," Blake said. "But we need to get the hell up out of here. I don't know who gave Bliss a shot of gin, but she is lit. And you know that doesn't bode well for us."

Paityn shot to her feet. "Is she okay?"

"Rissa and Rick have her, but it's time to go. Now."

"I'm sorry," Paityn told him. "I should probably go."

Bishop stood. "It's cool," he assured her. "I'll see you soon."

She grinned. "Can we hit pause on this conversation?"

He nodded. "How did you get here? Do you need a ride home?"

Paityn glanced at Blake. "If you don't mind the slight possibility that my sister might hurl in your back seat."

"I don't mind. That's what detail shops are for."

"Thanks," she told him. "I appreciate it. This way, Rissa won't have to go out of her way."

With his hand on the small of her back, he guided them out of the crowded restaurant. Maybe he would be able to get them home safely and go to sleep without thinking about what would have happened if he'd been alone with the lovely Paityn Young. *Somehow I doubt that.*

Chapter 4

"*S*orry, I'm late." Paityn slid into the booth across from Bishop.

After their heated exchange at the Cuban restaurant, Bishop thought it might be best to set up their first meeting at a public place, in the afternoon. So, he'd suggested coffee at The Manor Café. Bishop had lived at Park Manor for two years and enjoyed the amenities the luxury building offered its residents. The café had often been his go-to place to get a good cup of coffee or even do a little work.

A smile tugged at his lips as he watched her settle in, setting her cup of coffee on the table and removing her laptop from her briefcase—even though he'd told her not to bring it. This meeting would be a quick setup meeting, as he thought it best to learn her expectations before they got started.

As if she knew what he was thinking, she offered, "I know you told me not to bring this." She opened her laptop, typed something, and glanced at him. "But I felt like I should take notes."

"No problem. I'm glad you could meet me on such short notice."

It had been a week since he'd seen her, by design. He needed a couple of days, away from her, to refocus his priorities. Because she was still his boss' goddaughter. He was supposed to help her, not seduce her.

But when she'd entered the café that morning, he realized one thing—time away from her hadn't really changed anything. She had the same effect on him today as she did last week. Whether it was afternoon or evening, whether they were at her home or at the café, whether she was wearing black lace or black jeans, he still wanted her. Which made his decision to stay away from her futile.

She took a sip from her cup. "I'm actually glad you called. I needed a change of scenery. I've been holed up in the house for the past few days since my sisters left, trying to perfect this cream I've been working on."

"Any luck?"

Sighing, she shook her head. "No." She tapped the table. "But I'm close. I can feel it."

"That's good."

"To be honest, I'm surprised you wanted to meet here. Especially given the subject matter."

He chuckled. "I figured we could spend some time going over how you want this process to go. What do you expect from me?"

She tilted her head, narrowed her eyes on him. "That seems like a loaded question, considering our last interaction."

"Point taken."

"I could say the same thing. When you didn't call me, I figured I'd misjudged everything."

There weren't many people who had rendered him

speechless, but the woman in front of him had done that multiple times in the short time he'd known her.

"I have to tell you," she crossed her legs, "I've never been in this position before."

"Having coffee?"

"You know what I mean. Listen, Bishop, we're both adults. There's no reason to beat around the bush. Last time we saw each other, there was some strong..." She nibbled on that bottom lip, the same one he wanted to suck into mouth. "Attraction. I understand, if in the light of day, you realized that we can't explore it." She did a cute little hand gesture, and he couldn't help but smile. "I mean, you do work for Uncle Jax and we don't really know each other. But I think it deserves a conversation because we're going to be working together on something very dear to me. I don't want anything to affect that."

"It won't," he said. "And I'm sorry."

"For what?"

"For being a punk when I really should have just asked you to go out with me."

Her lips parted. "Oh."

Leaning forward, he closed her laptop, laughing when she flinched. "You're beautiful. And I'd be lying if I said I wasn't interested. At the same time, I need to make sure you have what you need for your business. So, you tell me how you want this to go. Business? Or pleasure?"

Paityn sighed. "What if I said both?"

"Then, I would still want us to have a conversation about expectations."

"Okay," she said simply. "Let's talk."

They spent the next hour talking her business. Paityn already had a firm grasp on business structures, funding sources, and even tax law. She'd run a successful practice for years, after all. But what he found refreshing was her willingness to think outside the box and keep an open mind. She listened to his advice on improving her business plan but wasn't afraid to tell him if she didn't agree with his ideas.

The small manufacturing company she'd used to produce her first prototypes had already expressed interest in working with her. Paityn was hands-on. She'd designed her few products herself and wanted to develop several more. Her practical experience as a sex therapist coupled with her knowledge of the human body and chemistry background made her proposal stand out, demonstrating that she knew her shit. When all was said and done, he was sure she'd be able to find investors. He also knew Jax would be first in line to jump in, based on the conversation he'd had with his boss earlier in the week.

"Do you want to see it?" she asked.

He frowned. "See what?"

She glanced around their immediate area. "The B.A.D.," she whispered.

Bishop knew from reading her proposal that B.A.D. stood for Big Ass D. He wasn't particularly interested in seeing it, but it was part of the business, so he needed to be familiar with her design. Chuckling, he said, "Lead the way."

When they entered the penthouse, a blast of cool air hit his face. The place was spotless, almost like no one lived there. Instead of the smell of peaches and pork, it smelled like pine trees. As he followed her further into the house, he took a moment to look at the décor. She hadn't been there long, but he noticed little pieces of her throughout the house—the blanket on the couch, pictures on end tables, and new artwork on the walls.

"It smells like winter," he said.

She turned back to him, a small smile on his face. "I

burned my favorite candle before I came down to the café. It's fresh balsam." They stopped at the kitchen, where she lit the candle that was on the island. "Reminds me of Christmas." She grinned. "And what do you know about winter, Mr. California Man."

Shrugging, he said, "I've spent some time in Chicago."

"Really? I love Chi-Town."

"Me, too. I have family there."

"Cool. We do, too. Have you been to Michigan?"

"A few times. A friend of mine lives in Wellspring, Michigan. And I've been to Detroit a couple of times."

Her eyes lit up. "I love Wellspring. It's a beautiful, small town. Very homey." She eyed him curiously. "A *girl* friend?"

It was obvious Paityn wasn't about that playing games life, which endeared her to him. "Nah. My boy, Bryson. He went back there to bury his father and ended up staying. Now, he's married with kids."

"That's nice. My parents have hosted several retreats there."

Bishop was very familiar with Stewart and Victoria Young. Aside from the fact that they were both clients of the agency, he'd worked with Stewart on several deals. "I've golfed with your father. I have a great deal of respect for him."

Paityn beamed. "I love him. We video chat a couple times a week." She opened her fridge and pulled out two bottles of water, much like she'd done the first time they'd met.

He took the offered bottle. "So you're pretty close?"

"Very. I'm close to my entire family. Every year, around the end of July, my parents host a weekend retreat for couples. It's a family affair. My brothers and sisters come, and we help them out. It's always been an opportunity for us to showcase our businesses as well."

As Paityn talked, he learned that each Young sibling had an entrepreneurial spirit, with careers ranging from matchmaker and professional wingman to personal chef and private investigator.

"Once it's over, we all head to some destination," she continued. "We usually rent a house and just chill with each other. Aside from Christmas, it's my favorite time of the year."

"That's cool."

"What about you?" She took a sip of water. "Do you have any siblings?"

"A younger brother. He's a surgeon."

"Are you two close?"

"Yes. It took a while for us to get to the place we're at now. When we were younger, I couldn't stand him. He tried his best to get on my nerves."

Laughing, Paityn said, "I know how that is. I'm the second oldest of the group. They treat me like I'm their second mother. They're like my children, always eating my food, asking for stuff... It's crazy."

"And you just give them what they want, right?"

Her mouth fell open, before she barked out a laugh. "Damn, you figured me out. I do have a soft heart where they're concerned. I can't seem to tell them no. Especially the twins and my youngest brother."

"I get it. Believe me. My brother bought a house, knowing he knew nothing about renovations. I ended up working on it myself."

"Really? That's amazing. My brother, Dexter, loves to rehab homes."

"I love the work. My father made his living in construction. I learned so much from him."

Bishop had no idea why he'd even shared that with her. He didn't usually offer up so much about himself to anyone, let alone someone he'd met a week ago. For some reason, though, he felt comfortable with her.

"Does your father still do that type of work?" she asked, resting her elbows against the island.

Bishop sighed. "No. He died a couple of years ago."

Sadness clouded her features. For him. "I'm so sorry. I didn't mean to… I'm sorry to hear that, Bishop."

"It's okay." It wasn't, but what else was he supposed to say. "He lived a full life, loved my mother until his last breath, and gave his all to me and my brother. He was one of the best people I know. That will never change." That part was the truth.

Paityn reached out and took his hands in hers. His gaze dropped to them. "That's beautiful."

Nodding, he swallowed past a lump in his throat. "It is."

"I don't know what I would do in your shoes. I can't imagine it."

"It's definitely a process," he said simply. Bishop had never really talked about losing his father with anyone. He'd just pushed his way through his own grief to be there for Ma and Gabe. "But it's life."

"It is, but…" She shot him a sad smile. "It's hard. And it's okay to feel that."

"That's what they say," he muttered sarcastically. He'd heard it all from every person in his life. *It will be okay, it won't hurt this way forever, be grateful you had him for this long…* It sucked. Plain and simple.

"Seriously." She squeezed his hand. "And no one should tell you anything different."

"Thank you."

She smiled, once again stealing his breath with the beauty of it. In that moment, he couldn't hear or see anything but her. "So, are you ready?"

He blinked. "Ready for what?"

"To see my prototype?"

"Oh, yeah." He tried to play off the fact that he hoped she was *ready* for his lips on hers, his hands on her body.

They walked to the office, where she'd set up a makeshift lab, of sorts. "I do my work in here." She pointed to the table where several toys were displayed. Starting at the first one, she gave him the rundown of each of them, what they were for, and how she hoped to market them. "I'm also trying to perfect a clitoral cream."

Bishop clenched his hands into fists and tried not to think about her clit or his mouth on her clit. "Cool." He cleared his throat. "Have you thought about doing a focus group? Getting a few ladies together to see what you've done here and get some opinions on the products?"

"I have, actually. I should probably set something up like that soon. My sisters and Rissa have all weighed in on them. But it would be helpful to talk to someone who isn't related to me."

"You should definitely do that sooner than later. Before we start pitching to investors."

"I will." She let out a heavy sigh, smacked her palms against her legs. "So, the easy part is over. You've seen my products; we've talked about the business. Now, you mentioned having a conversation about a date?"

Bishop couldn't get enough of her. "I did."

"Does this mean I have to wait for our date to see you again?"

"No."

"Good. So…?"

"So, what?"

"Ask me out, for goodness sake."

He inched closer to her. Reaching out, he gripped the

hem of her shirt, rubbed his thumb over the bottom button. "I thought that was already a given."

"Not until you ask me officially." She cracked up, letting her head fall back. And, soon, he was laughing with her. She reached out, planting her hand on his chest. "I'm just kidding with you. Where are you taking me?"

The play on words made his fingers ache with a need to pull her into him and *take* her right there on the desk. Which was strange for him because he'd never had such a visceral reaction to anyone like this. It was almost instinctual, like his world wouldn't be right if he couldn't be with her, even though it wasn't rational.

"Paityn." He pulled her closer. "If you continue to ask me questions like that, I might end up telling you answers you're not ready to hear."

A slow, sexy smile formed on her lips. "Try me."

His lips were on hers within seconds, sucking, nipping, licking. *Shit.* The feel of her mouth on his, her tongue stroking his, her body against his made him want to drop to his knees and pray she'd never make him stop. But he knew he had to. If he didn't stop, they'd be fucking in a matter of minutes. If he didn't stop, he was sure everything for him would change. If he didn't stop, he'd never let her go. Because this wasn't a simple kiss. It was a promise of more to come.

———

If Paityn hadn't been there, she wouldn't have believed it. Never before had she been so attracted to a man to the point of distraction. And never before had she been left so needy, so horny, after a kiss that she had to force herself not to beg him to do her. At this point, she didn't care how it happened or when, she just wanted him inside her at the earliest opportunity.

Unfortunately, the kiss she'd shared with Bishop a mere few days ago didn't lead anywhere. Instead, he'd ended his delicious assault on her mouth with his lips, his tongue and his teeth, planted a respectful kiss on her forehead and told her he'd call her later. And while she'd talked to him every day, she hadn't seen him since that heated moment in her office. They'd scheduled their date for the weekend because he had business out of town, and she was frustrated. No, she was borderline angry—and horny.

"Girl, what are you going through?" Burgundy asked from the adjacent treadmill. They'd gotten into sort of a routine, meeting at the gym each morning and working out together. Today was cardio day. "You beat the shit out of that punching bag for twenty minutes and now you're running like you're ready to tackle someone to the ground. Who pissed you off?"

Paityn grunted, then grumbled a curse. "Bishop. Lang."

Burgundy gave her a side eye. "Bishop? He's cool as hell. What did he do?"

"Nothing. That's exactly what he did."

"Okay, I'm confused. If he didn't do anything, why are you mad at him?"

She glanced over at Burgundy. "Because."

"Hm." Burgundy gasped. "Oh. I think I'm starting to understand what's going on. You *want* him to do something."

"Exactly." Paityn picked up the pace, focused on her breathing. In and out, in and out. Then, let out another curse. "We've talked every day in some way. I've learned more about him, and I've told him stuff about me. But he's such a gentleman. And I don't have time for nice. I want dirty and sweaty and long. I want kisses and bites and doggy style. I want nasty."

Laughter echoed in the empty gym, and soon Burgundy was bent over cracking up. "Girl, you're trippin'."

"I'm not," Paityn argued, not breaking her stride. "I'm super grown. Maybe there was a time for taking things slow, like in my teenage years. But I don't believe in the ninety-day rule. If I'm feeling someone, I'm okay with sex on the first date. What I'm not okay with is being so damn turned on I have to get myself off multiple times to feel better."

"Woo wee." Burgundy held her stomach. "I'm cracking up at you."

"That is not funny." Paityn slowed to a stop and blew out a harsh breath. "I mean, what do I have to do? Throw myself on his dick?" she shouted. "I just need to have sex!"

Bishop walked into the gym and stopped in his tracks.

Oh no. Paityn glanced at Burgundy, who was standing there with wide eyes. "Bishop?" she croaked.

"Paityn."

She scratched her forehead and stepped off the tread-mill. Only she misjudged her step and nearly took an "L". Quick reflexes ensured she didn't roll on the floor and embarrass herself even more. But, damn. She was morti-fied. And Burgundy? Her friend was laughing her ass off, not in a subtle way either.

Bishop hurried over to her. "Are you okay?"

Paityn looked up at him and could tell by the amuse-ment in his eyes that he'd heard everything she'd said. "I'm fine." Except she wasn't fine. Her ankle was throbbing. "I might have twisted my ankle," she groaned.

By the time Burgundy stopped laughing and made her

way over to see if she was okay, the leasing manager had tears streaming down her face. "Are you okay, girl?"

Paityn glared at the other woman. She couldn't be mad at her, because it was exactly the type of reaction Blake would have had. Hell, if the shoe were on the other foot, she might have done the same thing. Unable to help herself, she let out a chuckle. "Girl, I'm glad I'm not really hurt."

"Hi, Bishop," Burgundy said. "I'm sorry, Paityn, but I can't help it. That shit was hilarious. Are you sure you're okay?"

Paityn nodded. "Yes. But I'm going to call it a morning. I need to go put some ice on this ankle before I can't walk tomorrow."

Bishop wrapped his arm around her waist. "I'll walk you up."

Glaring at Burgundy again for good measure, she waved and let Bishop help her home.

A little while later, she was on her couch, her leg resting on the coffee table.

"Let me see that ankle." Bishop set the ice pack down and slid a pillow under her ankle. His fingers brushed up against her leg as he slid her sock down.

Paityn tensed, wondering if she'd remembered to put on lotion. "Um, you don't have to do that. I can take care of it."

"It's cool. I know a little about twisted ankles."

He pulled the sock off. *Thank God.* No ash. And she was glad she'd went for a pedicure with Rissa the other day. He examined her ankle, squeezing it gently and moving it in a circle. It only hurt a little, so Paityn was sure there was no break or fracture.

He ran a thumb over the sensitive skin. "It will probably swell up. It's pretty red here."

"I know," she breathed, distracted by his touch.

She watched as he leaned forward, picked up the ice pack and set it on her. She winced at the cold against her heated skin. "Ooooh."

"Sorry," he whispered, pushing it against her skin lightly. "You should be okay in a few hours."

She picked up the remote and turned on the television. "Thanks for walking me home," she murmured, still unable to look him in the eye.

"No problem." He wrapped his hand around her calf. "Are you sure you don't want me to get you anything else? Hungry?"

As if on cue, her stomach growled. She dropped her head. *Can this morning get any more embarrassing?* "I guess I could eat."

"What do you have a taste for?"

"I can just get a bowl of cereal," she said, making a move to stand.

He placed a hand on her arm, stopping her. "I can make a bowl of cereal. But do you want something hot?"

She wanted something hot alright. Pinching her lips together, she shook her head. "No. You don't have to cook for me."

"I wasn't going to cook. I can order Door Dash or call down to the café and have them bring you something."

"Okay. I want hash browns with feta cheese, sausage links fried hard, and two eggs scrambled soft with cheese." She gasped. "Oh, grits."

He chuckled, picking up his phone. "Glad you still have an appetite."

"I love food."

"That's good." Bishop ordered breakfast for two from the café. When he ended the call, he turned to her. "Twenty minutes."

"Thanks." She rested her head against the cushion. "I guess we should probably address the elephant in the room."

He turned, pretending to look around. "Is there an elephant?"

She laughed. "You're funny. But you know it is."

He braced his hand on the back of the couch. "Okay, let's talk about it." He traced the line of her ear, then trailed his fingers over her jaw.

She closed her eyes and took a deep breath. "I know you overheard me at the gym."

Running a thumb under her chin, he said, "I did."

Paityn shuddered as he continued to wind her up with feather light caresses. "What do you think?" she whispered.

He leaned in, brushed his lips against her chin before he nipped the skin there. "You want to throw yourself on my dick." He licked the sensitive spot behind her ear. "Because you're super grown."

Paityn giggled. "I am."

"I agree." He sucked her earlobe in his mouth. "You're definitely a woman."

"I don't sleep around, if that's what you're worried about."

"I never thought you did."

"So what's wrong?" she asked.

"Nothing."

He kissed her then, drawing a low moan from her throat. *Or was that him?* She didn't know, she didn't even care. She just wanted more. But far too soon, he pulled back.

Paityn felt like she was in a haze, a cloud of desire that made her feel unhinged. "You keep making me want you more," she admitted.

"Good. Because I want you, too."

"Okay." She let out a soft breath.

"Don't be embarrassed. I don't think less of you for knowing what you want." He kissed her nose, both of her cheeks, her eyes, then her mouth.

"Oh God, you're killing me."

"Paityn," he murmured against her mouth, before placing a chaste kiss there. He pulled back, meeting her gaze. "I like you. A lot. I like talking to you, laughing with you. What's wrong with getting to know each other more before we sleep together?"

"Nothing. I guess."

"I want to date you, Paityn Young."

Paityn's heart shifted. He was so freakin' cute and sincere and everything she'd never had before. If he wanted to wine and dine her, show her how to be wooed by a man, she was all in.

"Okay," she said with a mock pout. "But can you woo me *after* you do me?"

He barked out a laugh.

"You think it's funny, but I'm so serious."

"You're silly." He placed a kiss to her forehead and pulled her closer.

"I hope you mean that in a good way." She snuggled into him and reveled in the feel of his arms around her.

"In the best way."

Chapter 5

"When I invite someone over for Netflix and Chill, I expect to get some. Not actually watch the whole movie."

Blake laughed. "What the fuckety fuckery fuck? I can't believe he didn't make a move."

Paityn giggled. "I know, right? Here I am trying to be a hoe. And there he is treating me like a lady."

"Ha!"

"Girl, he wants to date me."

Blake stopped filing her fingernails. They'd been on the video chat for five minutes, catching up. Paityn had given her sister the lowdown on Bishop. "I can't believe I'm saying this, because you know I'm not about that dating life, but let him. He's perfect for you."

Laughing, Paityn wiped the countertop off. It was cleaning day, and she planned to dust, mop, and shine every surface of the house. The first room was the kitchen. "We're going out tonight." It was their first *official* date. Bishop hadn't told her anything about his plans, just that she should dress to impress.

"Good. Dating is perfectly healthy."

"Who are you? And what have you done with my perfectly petty little sister?"

Blake sighed heavily. "I'm still here and petty as fuck. But, I really do think Bishop is good for you. From what you've told me, and what I observed, he's good guy. And you deserve a good guy."

Paityn nibbled on her lip. "It seems too good to be true. We've only known each other for a few weeks."

"Shit, that's long enough to know whether you want to let someone into your world—and your bed. Usually, red flags fly on the first day. You know that."

Paityn definitely knew that. When she met Philip all those years ago, she knew he was nothing but trouble. But she'd let her emotions rule.

"What are you going to wear?" Blake asked.

"I have no idea. Rissa said I should wear the black dress I bought last week, the one I showed you on our last call."

"Yass, honey. If he doesn't give it to you after he sees you in that dress, *that* will be a red flag."

"Well, let's hope he likes what he sees."

"I have no doubt. The way he looked at you at the restaurant… Girl, I'm telling you. He's hanging by a string. But I give him props for trying to be respectful."

"You're crazy."

"How is everything going for the business?"

"It's good. Over the last week, we've been fine tuning the business plan. Then, we're going to work on a presentation and try it out on Uncle Jax. He also wants me to do a focus group for my products. I invited some of the ladies I met in the building over to do that."

"That's cool." Blake blew at her nail. "Sounds like you're moving forward nicely."

"I am. That clit cream, though. It's… Oooh." Paityn shifted, feeling a tingling feeling in her core.

"What's wrong?"

Frowning, she eyed her sister on the tablet's screen. "I just… I'm trying out a new version of the cream and I might be having a… Oh."

Blake looked concerned. "Girl, maybe you should wash it off?"

Shaking her head, Paityn waved a dismissive hand toward the screen. "Nah, I'm fine." But as she moved around the kitchen and listened to her sister's update about the family, she knew that she wasn't fine. She was aroused. Extremely aroused. *Is the cream working?*

"Tyn?"

She stopped, let out a slow breath. "Huh?"

"What's going on?"

"Oh, nothing." She bent down to wipe the bottom of the fridge. Her yoga capris must have rubbed against her in some kind of way because… "Oh shit!" Paityn stood up abruptly and glanced at the screen.

Blake's mouth fell open. "You said the 's' word. Is that cream you tried on working?"

Paityn braced herself against the counter, moved her hips to the right and then the left. With each movement, her nerves sparked to life. "Oh my God. It's working." *Perhaps, a little too much?* "Oh," she moaned.

"Girl!" Blake moved her face closer to the camera.

"I can't talk anymore." She squeezed her thighs together. "I have to go."

"What? Why?"

Because she was going to come. Or she wanted to come. *Semantics*. But she knew she couldn't do it while on the phone with her sister. "Blake, I'll call you back. Later."

"Wait!" Blake screamed. "Send me some of that shit!"

"Bye." Paityn ended the chat.

As if her body were on fire, she pulled off her shirt. She was just about to take off her tank and pants when she heard a knock. Glancing at the door, she thought about if she wanted to answer it. *What if it's important?* She closed her eyes tight. *Deep breaths, Paityn.*

She stood there a moment, hoping the sensations would die down. Another knock. *Shit.* Paityn rushed to the door. The sooner she answered it, the sooner she could be alone.

Paityn unlocked the door and opened it. Blinking, she said, "Bishop."

Bishop smiled, then frowned. "Hey. Are you okay?"

Flustered, and still hot as hell, she ran a hand through her hair. "Sure." She swallowed, pressing a hand against her rapidly beating heart. "It's early. Way early. I didn't expect you for hours." *Damn, he smells good.*

"I know." He studied her, with furrowed eyebrows. "Do you have company?"

Paityn shook her head. "I was just cleaning."

"I stopped by because I heard from Jax's assistant. He wants us to come to Atlanta for the presentation."

"Okay. Sounds good." She focused on a random spot on the wall behind him. Because she couldn't look at him and his hard body and his bedroom eyes. "Thanks for stopping by."

"And I just wanted to see you." Bishop reached out, brushed a finger over her cheek.

A mixture between a whimper and purr escaped her lips. "Oh, God." She licked her lips.

He stepped closer.

She retreated back.

"Paityn, what's going on?" He shoved his hands into his pockets.

"I'm going to come," she blurted out.

Bishop blinked. "Excuse me?"

She grabbed his arm and pulled him inside. Closing the door, she whispered. "I tested out a new batch of cream today and I'm hypersensitive right now. I know you said you want to date me, and I'm cool with that. Honestly. But you can't touch me. Not now."

His gaze swept over her. "You're so beautiful."

Paityn felt a blush work its way up her neck, to her ears and finally to her cheeks. She swayed on her feet. "You're killing me, Bishop."

"I don't want to kill you, Paityn." His voice was a low, dangerous whisper.

Or is that my mind playing tricks on me?

"But you are. You're killing me with your…" She flicked a hand in his direction. "With your you."

Bishop laughed. "How about if I—?"

"Leave," she finished. "I'm not mad. Trust me."

"No." He inched closer.

Paityn slumped against the wall and prayed she didn't slide to the floor. She peered up at him, fisting her hands into his shirt. "Bishop," she breathed.

"Fuck it." He gripped her chin and pulled her in for a searing kiss.

She tried to think past the desire rolling through her. But she couldn't concentrate on anything but the feel of his mouth, his hands. Every nerve ending was a tattered mess, her body burned with need. She was ready to explode.

When he pulled away, he searched her eyes as if she had all the answers. "Paityn?"

"Yes," she breathed.

For a second, she thought he was going to leave her there again, wanting him, needing him to put her out of her misery. But his lips crashed to hers again, and he lifted her in his arms and carried her to her bedroom.

He lowered her to the mattress, brushed his mouth against hers before he pulled her tank up and off, tossing it behind him.

"Shit," he murmured.

Paityn grinned. "The tank has a built-in bra."

"I like that." He traced one nipple with a finger before he took it in his mouth.

She held him to her as he switched his attention from one breast to the other, sucking greedily and sending her higher and higher with every kiss, every lick. "Oh, my. Oh, shit."

An orgasm crested within her, starting in her belly and spreading out through her body. She gasped as it thundered through her, stealing her breath. *And maybe my mind.* Moaning his name, she let it take over, let herself fall over the edge.

It felt like an eternity, but she knew it was only seconds before she was able to open her eyes. Bishop stared down at her, a soft expression in his dark eyes. "So beautiful," he whispered. He shifted, pulling away from her.

She grabbed his collar. "Don't you dare leave me here like this."

He laughed, dropping her forehead against her shoulders. She felt his lips against her skin, his tongue, then his teeth. "I'm not going anywhere," he murmured.

He sat up, and pulled his t-shirt off with one hand, giving her a full view of his massive chest. She traced the muscles of his stomach, trailed her fingers down his happy trail. "You're so hot," she breathed.

"So are you." He swept his hands up her legs slowly and pulled her shorts off. When his fingers grazed her clit, she arched off the bed. "I think you're ready to come for me again."

"Yes," she purred.

He massaged her until she gasped for air, then pushed two fingers inside her. It didn't take long before she was climaxing again, trembling as she came hard and fast.

Paityn's eyes popped open and a smile tugged at her lips. "I think... No, I know I want you inside me now." She removed his belt, unbuttoned his pants and pushed them off. His erection, straining against his sexy ass boxer briefs, drew her attention to it. Her mouth fell open. "Oh." She licked her lips and gripped him with her hands. "Impressive."

The corner of his mouth quirked up. He took her mouth in a lingering kiss. "Condom?"

Breathless and impatient, she pointed at the bedside table. "Drawer." It didn't take long for him to find her stash. He pulled one out, and she snatched it from him. "Let me." She slid it on and a beat later he was inside her.

He groaned. She moaned. They stayed like that for a minute, as Paityn adjusted to his size. But the need to complete reared its head and they began to move. Slowly at first, in and out. Paityn wasn't foolish enough to think this was just a booty call, or a fling. This was something else, something more. They moved together like they were destined to be this way, each of them giving and taking equally, each of them savoring every minute. Every second.

The pace picked up as they raced toward the edge. They came together, her screaming his name and him muttering a strained curse against her skin.

Once she could breathe again, Paityn squeezed his hips with her legs. "You're good at this." She grazed her fingers over his scalp.

She felt the tremble of his laughter against her. He

glanced up and kissed her chin. "It's that dope energy I was telling you about."

Paityn laughed. "Well, I'm glad you let me have some of that."

———

Bishop had spent the past twenty-four hours inside of Paityn. Well, not the entire day. They took a few breaks— and they had to eat. All of his plans for their date flew out the window when she'd answered the door, looking flushed, flustered, and so damn adorable. And when she'd told him why? He couldn't help himself. He couldn't walk away.

Now, he was behind on his schedule. He'd canceled his Saturday afternoon meeting with a client, was a no-show for breakfast with Gabe this morning, missed several calls from Ma, and just had to text the realtor he'd hired to sell Rod's house that he would be late.

It wasn't like him to blow off an entire day of meetings. Not to mention, he'd yet to open his work laptop. He hadn't even thought about checking his emails. The only thing he wanted to do was Paityn.

But it was more than sex. They'd talked, about everything and nothing. He learned more about her siblings and why she'd chosen sex therapy as a career. Paityn had even shared with him a few things about her marriage and divorce.

She had a way of getting him to reveal things he'd never told anyone else. And sometime between the slappin' lunch she'd whipped up and a late afternoon shower, he'd told her about Rod. Paityn had let him talk. Then, she'd climbed on top of him and rode him so long and so hard, he couldn't think straight. Surprisingly, it was exactly what he'd needed and he felt better for it today.

The realtor texted him back, asking to reschedule. Bishop typed out a quick response, but before he could hit send, a call came through. From Jax. On a Sunday afternoon.

Bishop answered the phone. "Hello, Jax. How's it going?"

"Bishop," Jax responded. "I'm good. I know it's Sunday, so I won't keep you long. Just checking in. It's been a while. How are you?"

"I'm fine. I have several things to keep me busy."

"I know it's been a tough couple of years for you. And I wanted to make sure you knew that I'm here to support you. Whatever you need."

Since Bishop had been at the agency, Jax had always been more than his boss. He was a friend, a mentor. He genuinely cared for his employees and proved it every day with how he led the company, how he interacted with his staff. Which was why Bishop would always be loyal to Pure Talent.

"I appreciate that."

"No, I appreciate you. Your work is impeccable. I never have to worry about the details. Which is why I wanted you on Paityn's project."

"Thanks."

"I don't have to tell you how important my goddaughter is to me. I know you'll take good care of her."

Bishop wondered if the type of care he'd given Paityn all night counted. But somehow he doubted it. "We're making good process." Clearing his throat, he added, "I talked to her about a trip to Atlanta in a few weeks." *Right before I took her on every available surface of your penthouse.*

He thought about telling Jax that he was interested in Paityn but decided against it. No use in saying anything before he knew what the hell they were doing. Against his better judgment, he'd skipped the first date and fast tracked the sex. It wasn't how he normally did things, but he didn't regret it. And he wanted more—more of her, more of everything.

"Perfect," Jax said. "When I read the revised business plan you sent, I started thinking about partnerships with established businesses, product placement, and even the possibly of a small storefront business."

Bishop had thought about all the possibilities, too. He'd examined every possible scenario, studied how similar companies expanded their businesses. Because that's what he did for a living and he enjoyed his job. And he enjoyed Paityn.

"I'm sure you've already gone over all of this with Paityn," Jax continued.

"I have. I've also started to work on that Pure Talent project you told me about. Based on my preliminary research, I think it's a viable plan. I'd like to set up some time to discuss my findings with you. Maybe next week?"

"Sounds good. Okay, son. Ana is calling. We'll talk soon."

"I'll send a calendar invite."

"Great. Enjoy your Sunday."

Bishop ended the call. His phone pinged and he glanced down to see he'd received a text.

Paityn: *This clit cream... I think I have a winner. Tweaking some things. Will be ready for a new trial soon. Dinner?*

A string of laughing emojis came through. Smirking, he typed out his response.

Bishop: *What do you have a taste for?*

Paityn: *You. And a burger.*

Bishop laughed. For the most part, he hated texting. But he didn't mind texting her. Her use of GIFs and emojis always made him laugh, though. She'd confessed early on that she hated talking on the phone, even though she was cool with video chats. Something about removing earrings and overheated phones making her sweat.

Glancing at his watch, he calculated drive time to Ma's house and back, considering traffic and odd jobs his mother might spring on him.

Bishop: *7:00?*

The dots jumped around on his screen, then a GIF of Beyoncé doing a suggestive dance popped up on his screen.

Paityn: *See you soon. I'll be ready.*

Chapter 6

"And this is what you're calling it?" Kathi eyed the tiny bottle skeptically.

From the moment she'd decided to embark on this new venture, she wanted to brand her products differently. Hence, the company name and the B.A.D. For the clit cream she'd recently perfected, she'd decided on the name, *That Ish*. She figured the name was appropriate because it made her say a word she'd banned from her vocabulary for years. And since then, she'd said it several times.

"Yes," she replied, checking on the potatoes cooking on the stove.

After she'd started dinner, she realized she didn't have whole milk to mash the potatoes, so she'd run down to the café to grab a bottle. It was pure luck that she'd run into Kathi in the lobby on the way back up because she thought it would be a good idea for someone other than Rissa to try out her concoction.

"I got the name from my sister." Paityn laughed when Kathi opened the bottle and smelled it. "And it really is that shit."

Kathi laughed. "Girl, you crack me up." She glanced at her watch. "I better get out of here. I know you have to finish your dinner."

They walked toward the door. "Don't think too much. It works." Paityn wiggled her eyebrows. "Trust me."

Wrinkling her nose, Kathi shook her head. "I don't know, Paityn. This might be a little too much for me."

"You have to try it! It's research."

Kathi opened her mouth to reply, but a familiar knock interrupted her. Paityn knew exactly who it was. Pulling the door open, she couldn't help the grin that spread across her lips. He was a sight for sore eyes. *Lawd, my man is fine.*

"Hey, you," she said, trying to ignore the fact that she'd even thought he was *her man.* Because they'd yet to define their whatever it was. And she was good with that.

"Hey, Paityn." His deep, gruff voice always made her swoon. Right then, she wanted to mount him in the hallway. It had been three days.

Gosh, I love the way he says my name.

"I'll just go," Kathi said, slipping past Bishop. "I'll call you, girl."

Paityn waved at her friend. "Bye, Kathi."

Bishop followed her into the house. Seconds later, she was pressed against the wall being kissed so hard and good, her knees buckled. Far too soon, he broke the kiss and rested his forehead against hers. They stayed like that for a moment, while she caught her breath.

He leaned back and grazed his thumb down her cheek. "Miss me?"

Bishop had been out of town and she wanted to welcome him back with hot food and hot sex. Initially, she wasn't too bothered by his impromptu business trip because she thought it was a good thing to have some distance. They'd seen a lot of each other over the last several weeks.

Paityn quickly realized her bed didn't feel right without him lying next to her. "Oh yeah," she cooed, brushing her lips against his. "And if I wasn't in the middle of dinner, I'd show you how much."

He gripped her wrist when she turned to head to the kitchen, tugging her back to him and kissing her again. "What if I can't wait?"

"You're going to have to. Unless you want burnt meatballs and scorched potatoes." She winked, leaning up on the tips of her toes to nip on his chin before she headed to the kitchen. "And I have a special surprise. I have a peach cobbler in the oven."

He groaned and let her pull him toward the kitchen. "You're playing dirty."

"Not yet." She laughed when he raised a brow. "Dirty is for later."

They talked about his trip for a few minutes while she finished fixing dinner. And once she was done, he helped her carry the food to the table.

Bishop poured two glasses of red wine. "What have you been up to?"

"Work." She took a sip. "I had a full day of client appointments yesterday and I bottled the clit cream to send samples to my sisters and Rissa."

"Hopefully, you'll get good feedback."

They ate their dinner, chatting about a variety of things. And it felt comfortable, right. There was still so much they didn't know about each other, but every time he revealed something about himself, she listened intently. And she found herself telling him things she hadn't even told Philip.

Bishop set his fork down. "Wait, soap opera characters?"

She swirled her fork around her plate. "That's what I said. Tristan, me, Duke, Dexter, Dallas, Blake, Bliss, and Asa. All soap opera characters."

"Wow." He leaned back in his chair.

She got the same reaction every time she shared how her mother had chosen their names. Victoria Young had chosen to stay home with her children and had become addicted to the "stories". She used her favorite characters, actors, or shows at the time to name them.

"I know, right? No one would ever believe it, considering how smart and accomplished she is."

"The crazy part is I know all of those characters."

She laughed. "Really? You watch soaps."

"No. Well, I didn't want to. My mom did. Every day. She worked nights."

"They were good shows, at least then. I remember watching All My Children, One Life to Live and General Hospital with my mother."

"Yeah, my mom watched those. And Knots Landing. I remember her watching that. Oh, and Dynasty."

Paityn laughed. "That was mom's favorite. She will even watch old episodes now when she's on vacation."

They both cracked up, and Paityn realized she loved the sound of his laugh. Hell, she loved everything about him. The thought sobered her, and she stood. "How about dessert?"

He slid his chair back when she sauntered to the kitchen and cut a piece of the cobbler. Grabbing a spoon, she walked back over to him and straddled his lap.

Sweeping his hands up her thighs and under her skirt, he gripped her hips and pushed his erection into her core. "Mm." He hummed against her mouth. "You taste good."

"And you feel good."

"We can eat that dessert later, ya know?" He unbuttoned her shirt and pushed it off.

"Ah ah ah. No." Leaning back, she scooped some cobbler up. "You didn't eat my cobbler last time."

Bishop let out a heavy sigh and kissed her neck. "Paityn," he grumbled.

"Why are you so hesitant? I can cook."

"Oh, I know."

"So what is the big deal? If you don't like peach cobbler, just tell me."

"I love it. It's my favorite."

"Okay, then. One bite, then you can have your way with me." His tongue darted out to moisten his lips. She held a spoonful of cobbler against his mouth. "Open up," she sang.

He finally opened his mouth and she slid the spoon in. Bishop closed his eyes as he chewed the cobbler. She waited for him to say something, wondering if she should have tasted it first. Maybe she didn't put enough nutmeg in it. When he opened his eyes, he mumbled. "This shit is good." He kissed the corners of her mouth. "Just like you."

Grinning, she rolled her hips and giggled when he groaned. Bishop unhooked her bra and pulled it off. He placed a line of kisses over the tips of her breasts before he took a nipple in his mouth.

This time it was her that let out a low groan. "Oh, God." The spoon she held slipped from her grasp and fell to the ground. She nearly dropped the plate, but he grabbed it and set it on the table next to them.

Her panties were gone next, ripped right off her body, followed by his shirt. She lifted up a second so he could push his pants and underwear off, and then she sank down on him. Another groan pierced the air. It could have been him or her. She didn't care. She just wanted him.

She moved over him, grinding into him, taking him deeper with each thrust of her hips. Paityn was obsessed with him, with the way he made her feel, the way he seemed to know what she wanted before she did.

She closed her eyes as he whispered filthy, dirty things to her. Things that made her want to prolong the night. Hell, she would prolong the week, the year, if it meant she could be with him like this. *Forever.*

With their eyes trained on each other, they moved in sync as they raced toward the finish. He pulled her into a kiss, sucking on her tongue until she cried out. And she was done. She stiffened, breathing his name as her orgasm shook through her. And he followed sinking his teeth into her shoulder.

Paityn collapsed against him. "Bishop." She let out a harsh breath. "I really missed you."

She felt the rumble of his laughter against her and smiled when wrapped his arms around her. He brushed his lips against her brow. "I missed you more."

A moment later, she glanced up at him and wrapped her arms around his neck. "Thanks for trying my cobbler."

He kissed her. "Thanks for making it for me. I think I want to keep you."

Paityn laughed. "Well, if you keep giving me all that dope energy, I'm happy to let you."

———

Bishop walked into his mother's house to find Gabe standing in the living room, his eyes on the pictures on the wall.

His brother turned to him, shot him a small, sad smile. "What's up?"

Bishop closed the door and approached him. "What happened?" He glanced around the room. "Where's Ma?"

Gabe gestured toward the back of the house, where the bedrooms were. "In her room."

"Is she sick?"

His brother shook his head. "No. She's sad. Anniversary. It would have been their forty-fifth. Then, you know…"

Bishop dropped his head, as the familiar pain he'd tried so hard to move past welled up inside. His chest tightened. "Yeah."

That one word was all he could say in that moment. Bishop knew the date was coming. It was hard to forget, since his father was born on the 4th of July. He'd tried not to dwell on it, though. And the fact that his parents married a week before his father's birthday made this time of year especially hard on his mother.

He squeezed Gabe's shoulder. "You okay?"

Gabe wiped his face. "It's still hard."

"I know. I'll go talk to Ma."

Bishop made his way back to his mother's bedroom. Ma was lying on her back, staring up at the ceiling. He knocked. "Ma?"

She didn't look at him. "Hi, babe."

He entered the room and sat next to her on the bed. Reaching out, he squeezed her hand. "Ma, what's going on?"

Shrugging, she said, "When I married your father, we had so many plans. We wanted to travel, visit fifty countries together. But we didn't have enough time." Her voice broke and so did his heart. "We thought there would be time to do the things we always wanted to do. I know that

God knows all and sees all, but I miss him so much I can barely see through the grief sometimes."

The unshed tears in her eyes finally fell, streaking down her face and onto the mattress beneath her. "We had planned to go to Florence on our forty-fifth anniversary," she continued. "I wanted to see Michelangelo's *David* and he wanted to eat some of that authentic Italian food." A weak chuckle burst forth. "You know your father could eat."

Bishop laughed. "He sure could. We had to hide the ribs from Pops every holiday."

"And the pound cake." Ma finally sat up. "Oh, babe." She caressed his cheek. "You remind me of your father. He had a calm about him that put everyone around him at ease. When he walked in a room, I knew everything would be okay."

Bishop stared down at his hands. His throat burned and his vision blurred.

"I miss him, too, Ma."

"It doesn't seem fair sometimes." She let out a heavy sigh. "But like I always told you, we can't question God."

He didn't understand that concept. Yet, he'd heard it countless times since his father died. But he had plenty of questions, needed so many answers. Starting with why. Why did his father end up with lung cancer when he never smoked a cigarette? Why did his father have to be in so much pain? Why didn't his father survive when so many people were able to live full lives after cancer?

"I don't mean to burden you with my pain. But sometimes the grief is too much."

"Ma, don't. You can always talk to me. I'll always listen."

When the doctor had given them the grim news that his father's cancer had spread and there was nothing left to do, Bishop was devastated. But Pops had immediately started planning, ensuring they knew where his life insurance policies were and even writing parts of his own obituary so they wouldn't have to do it.

One day, towards the end, Pops had asked Bishop and Gabe to come over for breakfast. They'd shared food and had a few laughs. Then, they'd cried, because they knew it was one of the last times they'd be together like that. Pops had instructed them to take care of each other and their mother and they'd both vowed to do so.

"And we can still celebrate," Bishop said. "We can celebrate his life."

Her eyes lit up. "With dinner together? All of us?"

Nodding, he smiled. "All of us."

"I love you, son."

He hugged his mother and tried not to drop a tear. "Love you, too."

Ma jerked back. "Where have you been? I've been calling you."

"Ma." Bishop chuckled. "I had to go out of town."

"Yeah, last week. You usually stop by when you get back from a business trip. Gabe had to hire someone to come in and fix the ceiling fan."

It had been a few days since he'd returned from his trip. And he'd spent every night with Paityn. She'd driven him to distraction. "I've been working."

Ma eyed him skeptically. "Boy, who do you think you're talking to? I know better. You met someone didn't you?"

He blinked. "Why do you say that?"

"Because I've known you all your life. You don't typically miss my calls, and if you do, you call me right back. The last couple of times I've called you, it took hours for you to call me back. You never miss a Sunday visit, and you don't go out of town and not stop by to see me when you get back. So that leads me to believe that you're *seeing* someone important."

"Her name is Paityn," he admitted, chuckling when his mother clapped and let out a delighted yelp. "She's... I don't know. I like her."

"You like her?" She grinned. "What does that mean exactly?"

He shrugged, rubbed a hand over his head. "I like her. We've been seeing each other for a few weeks."

"I knew I loved your father after two weeks." He'd heard the story many times in his life. His parents had met at church, during a revival. And the rest was history. "It doesn't take long to know if someone is the one for you."

Bishop had always thought insta-love was a myth, something that happened in romantic comedies or on the soaps his mother watched. Or, in his parents' case, as an exception to the rule. He didn't think it was possible to meet someone one week and love them the next. But he knew that Paityn was important to him. He already cared for her deeply, he already thought about a future with her.

"We'll see, Ma. For now, I'm just going to take things as they come."

Ma nodded. "Okay, son. But when I call you, you better pick up the phone."

Laughing, he pulled her into another hug. "I promise."

A few hours later, Bishop walked into Paityn's place. "Hey," he said when he saw her sprawled out on the couch, wrapped in the soft blanket she kept in the room.

"Hi." She grinned. "I didn't expect you so soon."

He climbed onto the couch with her and wrapped his arms around her. "Ma wanted to turn in early. What are you watching?"

"Crime tv."

Chuckling, he kissed the skin beneath her ear. "You and those crazy shows."

"I can't help it. I love to figure out who did it." Bishop buried his face in her neck, and she craned around to face him. "Are you okay?"

He smoothed two fingers over her furrowed brows. "I'm good."

She shifted a little more and rubbed her fingers over his cheeks. "Sure?"

"My mother had a bad day. She was emotional. My father's birthday and their anniversary are right around the corner."

Her expression softened. "I'm so sorry, baby."

"I don't know what to do," he confessed. "I want to be there for her, but she wants her husband. She misses him."

"I can understand that. How many years would they have been married?"

"Forty-five."

"Long time."

"Yeah."

"Are *you* okay?" she repeated.

"I'm worried about her."

"I'm sure you are. My heart goes out to her. But, Bishop, he was your father. His birthday approaching is probably hard for you, too. It's bound to stir up painful emotions. Right?"

He rested his head on her chest and squeezed her. "Yeah."

"You've had some hard hits. First your father, then Rod. You're strong, no doubt. But you're human. And I hope you know that you can be any way you need to be with me. You can say anything you need to say to me."

He hugged her tighter. "I miss him so much." A tear escaped and he sniffed.

Paityn wrapped her arms around him, held him to her. "I know." She kissed his forehead. "I know you do."

They stayed like that for several minutes, holding each other. Bishop didn't want to move. He wanted to lie there with her forever.

"You should celebrate your father on his birthday," she suggested.

"We are. We're having a big dinner with all of his favorites."

"Good. That should be fun."

He lifted his head, peered into her eyes. "Come with me."

Paityn's mouth fell open and her body tensed. "What?"

"I want you to come with me, meet my mom and my brother."

The visible change in her gave him pause. He tilted his head. Her eyes were suspiciously bright, damp. *Is she going to cry?* Averting her gaze, she slipped out from under him and stood.

"Paityn?"

"You want me to meet your mother?" She nibbled on her thumb. "I'm not sure it's the right time. I mean, it's your father's birthday. Family time. I don't want to intrude."

He stood and approached her. Squeezing her shoulders, he said, "It's not an intrusion if I invite you."

"Bishop, we're still getting to know each other. We haven't defined what we're doing. And it's your mother. Meeting parents is huge."

"I already know your parents."

"Right, so that doesn't count." She peered up at the ceiling, before meeting his gaze again. "I'm not ready. So, I'm going to say no."

Bishop nodded slowly. He couldn't believe the turn

their conversation had taken. One minute she was comforting him, making him think they were on the same page, telling him that she'd be there for him. And the next minute, she was… He didn't even know what this was. He knew he didn't like it, though.

"Okay," he said simply.

"Okay," she repeated.

Paityn walked into the kitchen, leaving him in the living room. Maybe he'd misjudged the entire situation. Obviously, he wanted something from her she wasn't ready to give. As much as he cared for her, he wasn't sure he had it in him to wait for her to realize that this wasn't a casual fling. And he didn't want to play himself by pretending it was just to be with her.

Chapter 7

"*I* messed up." Paityn stirred the vegetable dip she was preparing for the B.A.D. focus group and poured it into a small serving bowl.

Rissa set her purse down on a small table and joined her in the kitchen. "What are you talking about?"

The other ladies would be there in about an hour, but she'd called Rissa to come early—so she could tell her friend about her mistake. Panic welled up inside of her as she thought about her last interaction with Bishop, when she'd basically told him they weren't what she knew they were. When she'd turned down his invitation to a family dinner for a stupid, selfish reason that she didn't even understand now.

Sighing, she poured a healthy amount of wine into her glass. "Wine? I need wine for this conversation."

Rissa nodded. "Paityn, girl, what's going on?"

After she poured her friend a glass of Riesling, she padded to the den and plopped down on the couch. "Oh, I can't believe what an idiot I am."

ELLE WRIGHT

"What did you do?" Rissa took a seat on the chair next to the couch, setting her glass on an end table.

Taking a gulp of her drink, Paityn turned to her friend. "Bishop… I think I hurt his feelings. No." She shook her head. "I *know* I hurt him. And I'm sick about it."

"Oh, boy." Rissa sipped from her glass. "What happened?"

Paityn explained everything, starting from the moment he'd arrived at her house the other day and ending at the way he'd looked when he left. A smile that didn't reach his dark eyes. A forehead kiss instead of the usual long, lingering kiss to her lips. He didn't spend the night, like he'd done most nights since they'd started their…*What the hell are we?* He'd promised to call her—which he'd done a few times since that night—but one-word responses and awkward silences had replaced the normal comfortable conversations she'd grown to expect.

There was no doubt he'd taken what she had said to heart. Now he had pulled away from her. Because she'd hurt him. Because she'd basically disregarded his feelings. Because she'd discounted everything that they'd shared with each other, that they were to each other. *For what?* Some crazy notion that it was too soon to make a step that seemed so natural? Why wouldn't he invite her to his mother's house? She'd told him he could depend on her, that she'd be there for him. And when he asked her to be there, she fucked up.

Rissa stared at her incredulously when she finished, her mouth hanging open.

"Don't look at me like that," Paityn grumbled.

"When did this happen again?"

"It's been a few days."

"And you haven't seen him?" Rissa asked.

"No. I've talked to him, but he's been busy." *Avoiding me.*

"He was supposed to work on his friend's condo, get it ready to sell."

That was the truth. Bishop had already planned to spend the last few days getting Rod's condo ready to put on the market. They'd talked about it a while back. Still, it was weird he hadn't stopped by. She'd gone to his place yesterday, but he wasn't there. Bishop said he didn't play games, but deep down, she knew he'd purposefully put some distance between them. And she didn't blame him. After how she'd acted, she wouldn't be surprised if he walked away for good.

"Well." Rissa blew out a breath. "I don't…" she pursed her lips. "I just can't even believe how wrong you are."

Paityn expected this, she knew her friend would tell her the truth. No sugarcoating, no sympathy. Just plain truth. "But we haven't defined what we're doing," she mumbled. "Technically, it's not a relationship."

Rissa let out a humorless snicker. "Girl, please. It *is* a relationship."

It is. She'd known it then. She knew it now. Clearing her throat, she said, "I know."

"What I don't understand is… what's the big deal? It's dinner."

Paityn stood, paced the room. "I don't know. When he asked me, I just panicked. My entire relationship with Philip flashed through my mind in a matter of seconds."

"But Bishop is not Philip. He's not a punk, he's not a cheater. And he might love his mother, he might support her, but he's not a mama's boy."

Paityn had battled with Philip's meddling mother for much of their marriage and knew that was part of the reason she'd panicked when Bishop asked her to meet his mother. Only a small part, though. Mostly, her reaction had more to do with her own fears than anything else.

"Rissa, I hear you. But it's not like we've known each other for long. It's like we're speeding toward this destination that—"

Her friend held a hand up. "Enough of the excuses, Paityn. You know what? You're hiding."

Paityn gaped at her friend "What? I'm open. I'm not hiding."

"You are," Rissa insisted. "You have been since the divorce."

Dropping her head, she took a deep breath. "I'm not." Her reply sounded weak to her own ears.

"You've spent years teaching others how to have successful relationships, but you're scared to step out there again. That's your little secret."

"I'm the one who initiated this," Paityn argued. "I basically threw myself at him."

"For sex. That's the safe choice. Fuck and go. You act like you want someone in your life, but you keep coming up with all these reasons for why this won't work. First it was because of you may not be here long, now he's moving too fast by asking you to meet his mother. What is it going to be tomorrow? You don't like the way he drinks? Or how he sings in the shower?"

"Don't. I'm not like that."

"You are. I'm your best friend. I've watched you over the last month. I've watched you fall for him in a genuine, sincere way. Don't ruin that for a bunch of bullshit excuses that don't mean anything in the long run. They're just masking the fact that you're scared. You know this!"

Paityn did know that. She recognized it was all on her, not Bishop. He was too good to her, too perfect for her. She knew she was scared, but… *how can I not be?* She already liked Bishop more than she'd loved her ex-husband.

"And like you tell me," Rissa said, "like you tell your sisters, get over that shit. Fix it. Or you will regret it."

Paityn's eyes burned with fresh tears. One fell from her eye, and she wiped it away. "What if…" her voice cracked.

Rissa approached her, dashed more tears from her cheeks. "Don't do this to yourself. Yes, it's moving fast. Yes, you haven't known him that long. But so what. You make your own rules for your life. Who cares about convention? I know I don't give a fuck about what anyone thinks about me or my relationship with Rick. My friend Paityn never used to care either."

Paityn dropped her head to her friend's shoulder and hugged her. "You get on my nerves, telling the truth and all."

Rissa laughed. "That's what we do. Better me than those sisters of yours."

Paityn giggled. "Don't I know it."

She knew what she had to do. She needed to talk to Bishop as soon as possible. Before it was too late.

———

A chorus of laughter pierced the penthouse. The focus group slash sex toy party was in full swing. Paityn had plied her friends with good liquor and good food. Now, they sat in front of her table of goodies, listening to her presentation.

Paityn held up her favorite product. "This Big Ass D is my pride and joy."

"Oh, shit." Burgundy held out her hand. "I need an up close view."

Paityn handed it to her. "I was inspired by a dick pic I got on this dating site I joined for my sister."

"And you didn't block him?" Teegan asked.

"Hell. No." Paityn laughed. "Well, eventually—after I had hot phone sex and saved the pic. Then, I blocked his ass. I used it to design my big baddie because I thought his peen was so pretty." She shrugged. "Either that or I was just super horny."

The ladies cracked up. Paityn wanted to be relatable to any woman she talked to about sex. It wasn't unusual for her to sprinkle bits and pieces about her own sexual experience—or stories from her sisters with their permission— with attendees of her workshops and in her published work. She hadn't had a lot of partners, but she'd had a lot of sex. And she used strong language with her clients, always adding a disclaimer for new clients or workshop attendees beforehand.

"When I met with the manufacturer," Paityn explained, "I thought about women who wanted to mount something. I knew a regular dildo wouldn't do."

"Let me see that thing." Sky snatched it from Burgundy and studied it. "Hm." She finished her shot of tequila. "I like this. I want to try this one."

Paityn had ordered several samples of each of her prototypes from the manufacturer. She grabbed one of the boxes from the table. "Here you go. Now, remember, I need feedback." She handed Sky the box and clarified, "*Specific* feedback."

Over the next hour, Paityn went through all of her products, taking questions and giving out samples. She let the ladies try *That Ish* by instructing them to rub a tiny bit on their hands and blow. The demonstration elicited a strong response from her guests.

Teegan raised her hand. "I'll take one of those."

Paityn grinned, tossing a brand new bottle toward her, who caught it. "Be careful with that," she warned. "I call it that shit for a reason."

"Girl," Kathi chimed in, "She's not lying."

"Right," Paityn agreed, "Ask me how I know?"

By the time her presentation was done, she felt good about her products and more than a little hopeful about her business. Rissa had been jotting down notes for her the entire time and she couldn't wait to read them—and debrief Bishop. The plan was to do her presentation as a ladies night event. But, he'd agreed to come by afterward. She wasn't sure he still planned to come, especially since she hadn't seen him in a few days.

As the ladies trickled out one by one, Paityn watched the clock. The demonstration went longer than planned. *He should have been here by now.*

"Are you good?" Rissa asked, after her last guest left. "I think you can count this as a success. Let's hope you get awesome feedback."

"I hope so." She plastered a smile on her face. For what, she didn't know. It was just Rissa. Her friend knew her well. "I'm sorry. I just... I hoped he would still come."

"It's a good thing he didn't come on time. Gave you more time to hang out with the ladies."

"True." She heard the door close and perked up. A few seconds later, Bishop rounded the corner. "Hey."

He smiled. It still didn't reach his eyes. "Hey." Glancing at Rissa, he said, "What's up, Rissa?"

Rissa hugged him. "Nothing much." Her friend looked at her with wide eyes and a toothy grin. She pointed toward the door. "On my way out," she added.

"I'll walk you out," Paityn said.

"No," her friend said. "Stay here. I can close the door on my own. Call you, girl." Rissa grabbed her purse and left.

When she heard the front door close, she turned to Bishop. "I didn't think you were coming."

"Why wouldn't I come?" He sat down. "We agreed to debrief after the demonstration."

"Right." The room descended into an uncomfortable silence. Admittedly, everything she'd planned to say to him seemed stupid now that she was face-to-face with him. She struggled to figure out how to start the conversation.

"How did it go?" he asked.

"Good."

Another stretch of tense silence followed. Paityn peered up at the ceiling. Rissa's words replayed in her mind. *Get your shit together.*

"I'm sorry." She walked toward him. "I was wrong. Instead of just telling you that, I buried my head in the sand." She sat down next to him. "The truth is I was... I'm scared."

His brows drew together. "Of me?"

"Kind of," she admitted. "Of us. Listen, I've told you a little bit about my marriage. But the gist of it is, I'm terrified to get hurt again."

His gaze softened. "How do you know I'll hurt you?"

"I don't." She hunched a shoulder. "I tried to convince myself that you would. Because that would mean I wasn't such a bitch for the way I acted. I told you to lean on me and then I didn't let you. I would understand if you never wanted to see me again."

The corner of his mouth lifted. "Thank you. I appreciate your honesty. I should probably apologize to you."

Frowning, she said, "You didn't do anything."

"I told you I didn't like games, yet I played one. The past few days, I stayed away from you without telling you why. That's not me."

"It's okay."

"It's not." He picked up her hand, cupped it in his. "One of the reasons I'm so attracted to you is that you're honest. Even the other day, you told me your truth. I didn't like it, but I didn't give you the same courtesy by telling you mine."

She shook her head. "No. I wasn't honest. I didn't tell you why. I made up an excuse."

"An excuse rooted in truth. You're scared. Honestly, I am, too. Which is why I stayed away, why I pulled back. Paityn, this is more than a fling for me."

"Bishop, I know. It's more for me, too." She nodded. "It is."

"If we're going to do this, we have to promise to always tell each other our truths, even if it hurts."

She lifted his hand, brushed her lips against his knuckles. "Okay. Even it's scary."

He pulled her into his lap and she wrapped her arms around his neck. "I missed you," she murmured against his neck.

"I missed you, too." He pressed his lips to her shoulder, to the sensitive spot below her ear, to her jaw, to her cheek, and finally her lips.

Pulling back, she smiled. "What time is dinner at your mom's? And what should I bring?"

———

"Junior!" Bishop stepped further into his mother's house and smiled as Ma waved them over. "Get in here, boy."

He glanced over at Paityn and noticed the nervous smile on her full lips. It had been a week since they'd made a promise to tell the truth and he'd probably already broken it. Because he was sure he was in love with her and had yet to tell her. Not because he was scared, but because he wasn't certain that was what he was feeling. Up until that point, he thought he'd been in love before. But nothing had ever felt the way Paityn made him feel.

Leaning in, he whispered against her ear, "It's okay, baby."

Paityn looked up at him, her big, doe eyes wide. His girlfriend was stunning, even when she was casual in ripped jeans that fit the curves of her body like a glove, a simple t-shirt, and a pair of strappy sandals. Her short hair was spiky and wild, like he liked it.

Nodding, she squeezed his hand. "I know."

Bishop led her into the house, which was filled with his extended family and smelled like heaven soaked in barbecue sauce. On the way to his mother, Bishop stopped to introduce her to several people. She shook hands, gave hugs, and even kissed babies on their cheeks.

"Hey, Ma." Bishop squeezed Paityn's hand. "Are you still cooking?"

Ma smiled and flung her arms around him, a wooden spoon in one hand and a napkin in the other. She kissed his cheek. "Almost done."

He tugged Paityn forward. "Ma, this is Paityn. Paityn, this is Ma."

"Hi, Paityn." His mother pulled his girlfriend into a tight hug. "I don't shake hands. I hug."

Paityn peered at Bishop as Ma embraced her, the nervous smile still there. The entire day, he'd watched her nerves get the best of her. She didn't eat breakfast that morning and had complained of a stomachache while she made the banana pudding they'd brought with them. On the way there, her knee had bounced like a basketball until he'd placed his hand over it to stop the movement.

Ma grinned at Paityn. "You're so pretty. Thanks for coming."

Paityn blinked. "Thank you for having me."

"I heard you gave my cobbler a run for the money," Ma said.

Laughing, Paityn said, "Did he tell you that?"

"Yes, he did." Ma gave him a sidelong glance. "He couldn't wait to tell me how good it was. Which is saying something. You'll have to let me try it one day soon."

"Definitely, Mrs. Lang."

"Call me Ma."

"Okay, Ma." Paityn's shoulders dropped and she turned to him and blessed him with a smile that took his breath away. That was the moment he realized that she no longer needed him. That thought was further cemented when Paityn asked, "What can I do to help?"

Ma winked at Bishop. "I like her already, Junior."

Bishop laughed. "I knew you would." He kissed his girlfriend. "I like her, too."

Paityn shot him a wobbly smile. "Thank you. But you can go now."

Before he left the kitchen, Paityn jumped into action, offering help in any way she could. While they finished dinner, he brought Gabe, Cynthia, and the girls in to meet her.

Cynthia shot him a mock glare. "You finally decided to bring her around, brother-in-love."

Bishop wrapped his arm around Paityn. "Don't make me regret it, sis. No old stories. Or I'll be forced to tell her about your unfortunate Christmas pageant incident."

"Oooh." Gabe barked out a laugh. "That *would* be unfortunate."

"Shut up, fool." Cynthia smacked Bishop's arm, playfully. "You were sworn to secrecy."

"What happened at the Christmas pageant?" Paityn asked.

"Get out of here," Cynthia pushed him toward the door. "And take Gabe with you."

Dinner was served around six o'clock. Ma had outdone herself making all of Pops' favorites—ribs so tender he could pull the meat off the bones, creamy macaroni and cheese, juicy steak bites, and greens.

Halfway through dinner, Paityn had leaned over and asked him if he thought Ma would share her seafood pasta salad recipe with her. Since he knew his mother to be extremely secretive with her recipes, he was shocked when Ma spoke up, telling Paityn she would happily share her recipe if she shared her secret for the banana pudding she'd made.

People were packed in every room of the house. It was so crowded that Paityn had eaten on his lap because there was no room at the table. His family seemed to love Paityn. She'd joked with his mother and aunts, played cards with his cousins, and had a few shots with his uncles. She'd fit right in.

Later on, everyone ventured to the backyard where they paid tribute to his father. Tears were shed as, one by one, family members shared fond memories of a great husband, father, uncle, brother, and friend. Paityn had stayed by Bishop's side the entire time, offering him silent comfort as he gave his own speech. The night culminated with the release of several Chinese lanterns.

"I had a good time tonight." Paityn climbed into bed and fell back onto the mattress once they'd made it back to her place. She rubbed her stomach. "I'm so full. I couldn't stop eating. I probably gained three pounds just eating ribs."

He crawled over her, placing a kiss to her stomach, the tops of her breasts, and her lips. Rolling over to his back, he pulled her to him. "Ma really put her foot in that food. Dad would have been happy."

She giggled, snuggling into him. "I'm so glad I went. Your family is pretty amazing. Everyone was so welcoming, real, funny, and loving. Made me feel like I was at home with my family."

Bishop kissed her brow. "They loved you." *I love you.*

"You think so?" She lifted herself up on her elbow. "Because I loved them."

"Oh, yeah. My mother thinks you're perfect for me." *I do, too.*

"Good." She nibbled on her bottom lip. "Because I agree. I'm perfect for you."

He tickled her, laughing when she broke out into a fit of giggles. Rolling her onto her back, he kissed her, deeply and possessively. "Thank you for being there today. It meant a lot to me." He circled her nose with his. "You mean a lot me." *I love you.*

She wrapped her arms around his neck and brushed her mouth over his. "I love this. I love being with you."

He peered into her eyes. *Just say it.* "Me, too." He nipped at her flushed skin, enjoying her soft gasp. Slowly, he kissed his way down her body, removing her clothes as he did. Hooking a finger under the waistband of her lace panties, he pulled them off. "I want you, Paityn."

The cute little purr that burst from her lips when he blew on her core, made him want to sink inside her and stay there forever. He nipped at the sensitive skin of her inner thigh.

"Bishop," she moaned. "Please."

Inhaling her sweet scent, he ran his thumb over her clit before he took it in his mouth, sucking and licking her until she begged for mercy. It never took long when he loved her like this. Soon, she screamed out his name as her orgasm shuddered through her.

He kissed his way back up her body, paying extra attention to her nipples, grinning when she climaxed again. Bishop loved how responsive she was to him, how open, how ready she was for whatever he wanted to give her.

"Paityn?"

Her eyes popped open, and a slow smile formed on her swollen lips. "Yes," she breathed, stretching like a satisfied cat.

"Throw yourself on my dick."

Giggling, Paityn helped him remove his clothes and climbed on his lap. Seconds later, she eased herself down onto him.

"Shit."

They laughed, realizing they'd said the same word at the same time. He wrapped a hand around the back of her neck and pulled her to him, kissing her with everything he had. The need to move overtook him, and he pushed himself into her. He gripped her hips as she rode him, loving him. They were so good together, so natural with each other. He realized he was lightweight obsessed with her.

She pushed, he pulled. He groaned, she groaned. They were in sync, in tune with one another in a way he'd never been with any lover. He couldn't get enough of her. He wanted to be like this with her always.

"Bishop," she gasped.

He grunted, placed a wet kiss to her mouth. Then, he flipped her over, chuckling at her delighted yelp.

"Shit," she murmured, when Bishop thrust into her deeper, harder. "Don't stop."

"Never."

As they set a pace of slow and fast movements, he

knew he wouldn't be able to last much longer. He needed her with him, though. Hooking his arms under her legs, he tilted her bottom up and pressed into her one last time. She came then, repeating his name over and over again. And he was right with her.

Moments later, Bishop collapsed onto his back. She rolled into him, nipped at his chin. "Baby?" She kissed his neck.

Running his fingers through her hair, he said, "Yes?"

"Let's always be like this."

He leaned back to meet her gaze. There was no doubt about it. Bishop was in love with her. Pressing his lips to hers, he pulled her closer. "Okay." He swallowed. Hard. "Always."

Chapter 8

"*W*hat about this?" Paityn held up a black dress.

Bishop glanced up from his laptop and shook his head. "Not for a workshop."

She pouted. "But you liked this dress when I wore it last month."

"I liked taking it off of you, too. But it's a little too revealing for the occasion. You're there to help the couples, not distract the husbands."

Seconds later, he ducked as the dress came flying toward his head.

Laughing, he shook his head. "Seriously. Wear a suit and call it day."

It had been ten minutes of this, her holding up dresses and him sitting there watching her. Bishop finished up an email to Jax. Due to his boss' schedule, they'd rescheduled their meeting several times. They'd just returned from Atlanta a few days ago. While in Georgia, they'd met with Jax and had dinner with her parents, who were in town on business. Now Paityn was packing for her trip to Michigan.

The past several weeks had been a whirlwind of meetings and business dinners as they geared up to start B.A.D. Toys. Paityn had decided to launch on a smaller scale, by opening a small store. He'd been working long hours to secure a location in the area. So far, she had several investors which made the process easier.

Bishop had chosen to invest in her vision, using a portion of the proceeds from the sale of Rod's condo. The rest he'd donated to several charities in Rod's name, including two that meant a lot to his friend, the American Red Cross and Big Brothers Big Sisters.

Paityn disappeared into the walk-in closet and emerged minutes later with three business suits. "I think suits are so stuffy. I want to be relatable. And I want to be comfortable." She held up a black suit and tossed it back on the bed. "This sucks. I've never had this much trouble packing. Forget it. I'll wear this blue suit with the lace cami underneath."

"Good choice," he murmured, skimming a document he'd received from a co-worker.

"Are you still planning to come to the wedding?" she asked.

One of Paityn's cousins was getting married, so her family planned to attend after the retreat. She'd asked him to come to Detroit and attend with her. "I'll be there."

Paityn sauntered toward him, a grin on her face. Leaning closer, she kissed him. "Good. I was thinking we could get a room at the hotel, so we don't have to drive all the way back to Ann Arbor after the reception."

He set his laptop down and pulled her on his lap. "Sounds like a plan. You can wear that black dress to the wedding?"

"Hell no. I bought a new dress for the wedding."

Bishop flicked the top button of her blouse open.

"Whatever you want. As long as it's easy to remove. Two weeks is a long time, baby."

She traced the line of his nose. "I know. But I'd already planned the trip before I met you."

When Paityn had told him about her plans, he hadn't expected her to be gone so long. But he knew she had a lot to do back home. In addition to her parents' retreat and the subsequent family getaway, she'd scheduled a few client meetings and a workshop. The wedding was at the tail end of the long trip.

"It's okay." He placed a line of wet kisses up her neck and bit her earlobe softly. "I have a lot of work to do at the house."

Bishop had recently closed on a house in his mother's neighborhood, which he'd planned to renovate and rent. He already had a potential renter lined up, a young couple from Ma's church.

"I'll miss you," she said.

I love you. And, no, he still hadn't told her. They'd grown closer, spent time a lot of time together, but he still wasn't sure the timing was right. He'd assumed she wasn't ready to hear the words. But his reluctance also had something to do with the knowledge that if she didn't love him, it would probably wreck him. So despite the promise he'd made to be honest even if it hurt, he'd chosen to keep his feelings hidden to protect himself.

He nipped at her bottom lip before pulling her into a kiss. It wasn't long before her shirt was on the floor, but she broke the kiss and stood. "Baby," he grasped at the air as she stepped out of his reach.

Holding a hand out in front of her, she giggled. "Bishop, I can't. I have a plane to catch in the morning. I have to pack."

Grumbling a curse, he stood, grabbed a mound of her

clothes, and tossed them into an open suitcase. He zipped it up and turned to her. "See? Done packing."

She gaped at him. "You can't just throw my clothes in there like that. I have to organize, color coordinate." Paityn unzipped the suitcase and pulled the stuff out. "Some of these items have to be rolled up. And this skirt," she held up a black skirt, "goes in the garment bag."

Paityn refolded a pair of white jeans and set them on the bed. Frustrated, he hooked a finger and tugged at her belt, pulling her to him. She crashed against him, cracking up.

"Take a break," he said, pulling her belt off and tossing it behind him.

She gasped when it clanked against the mirror. Grinning, she said, "You could have broken the mirror."

"I didn't." Unzipping her pants, he pushed them over her hips. "Step out of these."

She did as she was told. "You're so bossy."

He removed her bra, then her underwear. Stepping back, he raked his gaze over her naked body, starting at her painted toes and traveling up her long legs to the apex of her thighs to her flat stomach and her full breasts. He brushed a finger over a turgid nipple.

"Beautiful." He stepped into her and turned her around suddenly. Her sharp intake of breath made him smile. Bishop wrapped his arms around her, cupping her breasts in his palms. Eyeing her in the full-length mirror, he murmured against her ear. "Mine."

"Yes," she breathed. "I'm yours."

"Good." He smacked her ass lightly. "Now, bend over."

———

Paityn sat behind her father as he spoke to a room full of

ELLE WRIGHT

couples about marriage. The annual retreat had been a success so far. Couples had come with open minds and willing hearts, and many had already referred other couples for the next retreat.

"See that lady right there?" Bliss leaned in. "In the blue sundress?"

Paityn swept her gaze over the crowd. "With the blonde hair?"

"Yes," her sister whispered.

The young woman had been an eager participant in Paityn's workshop and had even requested a private session. Her husband, though, had seemed to be indifferent to the process. "What about her?" Paityn asked.

"Her husband tried to hit on Dallas."

Paityn's mouth fell open.

"Close your mouth," Blake said.

Snapping her mouth shut, Paityn glanced at Dallas, who was sitting next to Blake, eyes on the crowd. "Really?"

Dallas nodded slowly, almost imperceptibly. Of all of them, Dallas had the best poker face. She barely reacted to anything and never let anyone see her sweat.

Shaking her head, Paityn sighed. "He's a bastard," she grumbled.

"Tell me about it," Bliss agreed.

Blake snickered. "It's cool. When I see him, I'll hit on him. Bust him in his fuckin' eye."

Bliss snorted, drawing their mother's attention. Victoria was seated next to her father, her legs crossed and her glasses perched on her nose. She eyed all of them in that "what the hell are y'all up to" way she always did when they were younger.

"You're in trouble," Dexter murmured from behind her.

"Shut up."

Paityn had enjoyed her time with her family. She'd used the opportunity to spend individual time with all of her siblings, her mom, and her dad. Then, she'd cooked dinner for the collective group. It was at that family dinner, that she'd told everyone about Bishop.

While in Atlanta, she and Bishop had gone to dinner with her parents, so they already knew about them. Shortly after they returned to California, her mother had called and told her she really liked Bishop for her. Her father had also chimed in, remarking how comfortable and happy she'd seemed.

Since she'd been in Michigan, she'd talked to Bishop every day and video chatted with him every night, even squeezing in few virtual sex romps. But she missed him. She missed falling asleep and waking up in his arms. She yearned to touch him, to kiss him, to love him. Because she *did* love him. She just hadn't told him yet.

"Hi, Mr. Young." A young woman stood up from the audience. This was the Q & A portion of the weekend, and they'd been there an hour fielding various questions from attendees. "You talked about loving someone where they are in your latest book. Can you expand on that a little?"

Paityn picked up her phone and snapped a picture of her father, while he talked. She loved to see him at work. He had such a calm demeanor, a melodic voice, and he immediately put people at ease.

Her brother Duke tapped her shoulder. "Hey."

Leaning back, she whispered, "What?"

"What's Bishop doing here?"

Paityn sat up, scanned the crowd. Sure enough, Bishop was seated near the back of the room. *What the hell?* She stood up, just as he did, raising his hand.

Her father smiled, but he didn't look surprised to see her boyfriend. "Ah, Bishop, did you have a question?"

"Oh, shit," Blake said.

Paityn stepped forward and Bishop's gaze locked on her. He smiled, then turned to her father. "Yes, I did. What if you love you someone, but you don't know if they're ready to hear it?"

Bliss awed. "Oh, Tyn."

Her heart hammered in her chest. *Did he…?*

Her father chuckled. "I can give you my personal opinion, then I'll give you my professional one." Turning to her, Dad smiled. Then, he stood. "My personal opinion is to always tell your truth. Even if you're not sure how the other person feels. But, usually, you can tell when someone loves you. Love is a verb. It's something you do, not something that is. Their actions tell the story. When you make the choice to love someone, you're choosing to accept them for who they are, to protect them, to be there for them. That's why the marriage vows are so important. They're more than words. They're promises."

"Thank you." Bishop walked up to the stage.

She walked to the edge of the platform, fully aware that everyone in the room was watching her. With wide eyes, she asked, "What are you doing here?"

"Attending the couple's retreat," he said with a shrug.

Jumping down from the stage, she gripped his wrist and pulled him out of the room. Outside the room, she turned to him. "Bishop, what are you—?"

His lips against hers effectively cut off her question. She gripped his shirt into a fist and kissed him fully.

It was official. Paityn was hopelessly, dangerously in love with him. He'd stolen her heart from the moment he'd walked into her house and pretended not to want her cobbler.

When he broke the kiss, he leaned his forehead against hers. "How are you? You good?" he asked.

"I'm good. How are you?"

"I love you. So, I guess that's good."

Paityn laughed. "You're crazy. You came to the retreat." She still couldn't believe it.

"For you. I promised to tell you the truth. And I didn't. So I figured I'd better rectify that. So, I came here to tell you how I felt."

Tears welled up in her eyes. "You love me." She blinked and the tears fell. He wiped them away. "That's good. Because I love you, too. So much."

"Don't cry, baby." Bishop kissed her cheeks.

She sniffed. "I'm not crying."

He laughed. "Okay. You're not crying."

Paityn hugged him. "You're so getting some as soon as this Q & A is over."

"When is that exactly? It's been going on for a long time."

She pulled back, unable to stop smiling. Because he'd come all the way there to tell her he loved her. And she needed to go ahead and call it a day so she could show him how much he meant to her. Like her father said, it was all about action. *Right?*

"Give me five minutes." She stepped up on the tips of her toes and kissed him. "I'll let them know I'm done for the day."

She turned to walk away, but he grabbed her, tugging her back to him. "Paityn?"

"Yes?"

"Let's always be like this."

Paityn's heart shifted full of longing for him, full of love for him. Only him. "Always."

Epilogue

"*M*rs. Lang?"

Paityn turned, smiling at her new husband. "Mr. Lang."

Bishop smirked, tugging her to him and into a kiss. "Any regrets?"

"Not one."

Bishop proposed during their Labor Day weekend trip to Miami. And they'd made it official two weeks later, tying the knot in her parents' backyard, surrounded by their friends and family.

They could have done the big wedding, big dress, and big reception, but Paityn didn't feel like going crazy over details. What mattered was their commitment to each other. What mattered was their promise to be there every day for the rest of their lives. Always.

"Ready?" he asked, holding his hand out. "They're waiting for us."

Her family had planned a small reception. *I guess we better show up.* She slipped her hand into his, smiling when he brushed his lips against her palm. "When you are? I love you."

Bishop brushed a tender kiss to her lips. "I love you, too."

Women of Park Manor

Her Forbidden Fantasy by Angela Seals
Her Essential Love by Anita Davis
Her Little Secret by Elle Wright
Her Undeniable Distraction by Sherelle Green
Her Passionate Promise by Sheryl Lister

Excerpt: Made to Hold You

DECADES: A JOURNEY OF AFRICAN AMERICAN ROMANCE

Prologue

April 1987
        Just say no.

Layla Johnson gripped the wooden bat in her hand and swallowed past the lump in her throat. As she stared at the townhome with the green door in front of her, she wondered how her life had taken such a drastic turn. Scanning the area, she watched strange people stagger out of the house, listened to the men and women milling around outside.

To an outsider, Prospect Woods might seem like a nice, quiet neighborhood—one of several in her hometown of Ypsilanti, Michigan. But to locals, it was anything but. Once the sun set, the apartment community turned into a den of thieves, prostitutes, and junkies. Layla never thought she'd have a reason to step foot inside the gate until she'd received a call from an anonymous caller telling her that she could find her husband, Lincoln, there.

Layla sucked in a deep breath, smoothing a hand over her stomach. In a few weeks, her son would arrive. But in a few minutes, her life would change forever. Over the past year all of her dreams, all of their plans, had gone up in smoke. Literally. Because the man that she'd promised to love forever had hurt her to her core. And because the love of her life had let his addiction destroy what they had spent years building. Gone were the hopes of a good life with her small family of four. The warmth of a love that seemed to shine so bright had turned to a bitter cold.

Layla had struggled with whether her marriage was worth saving. And every time she'd warred with herself, she'd ultimately decide it was—until a few days ago. Her husband, Lincoln, had been a no-show when she'd been rushed to the hospital with early labor pains. She'd cried for Linc as the doctors had rushed to her aid, as they attempted to stop her labor. But he didn't come, he didn't call. Fortunately, the doctors were able to stop the contractions, and she'd been released from the hospital with strict instructions to stay in the bed and avoid stress.

Walking into her empty home after her short hospital stay had hurt Layla, but she'd held it together. Realizing that Linc had taken her wedding ring and all of the money she'd hidden away for her maternity leave had gutted her. He'd made his decision. The drugs were obviously more important than her, than their children. The hard decision to walk away from her husband was devastating, but necessary. She had two innocent children to think about. Tomorrow, she would start a new life without Lincoln, but tonight she had to make sure he was safe. Once she did that, she'd make her move.

Layla felt tears well in her eyes, and willed them not to fall. Her hands trembled as she gripped the bat. She had no idea what she would find behind those doors. Was Linc still there? Was he still alive? Was he alone? So many questions ran through her mind on an endless loop. But now wasn't the time to get emotional. She had to get the job done. Letting out a slow breath, she gripped the wood tighter.

"It's okay, baby." Linc's mother, Martha, squeezed Layla's hand, offering strong support.

When Layla had received the anonymous call, the older woman was the first person she'd thought to call. Martha had been so supportive, had loved her like she was her own child. That's what the Wilson clan did. Once you were one of them, you remained one of them.

"I'm scared, Ma."

Ma offered her a small smile, but Layla knew it wasn't genuine. After all, there was nothing to smile about. Layla wasn't the only one hurting. Ma had suffered unimaginable loss as well. They all had. "I am, too. But when you came to me, I told you I could handle this on my own."

Layla shook her head. There was no way she could let Ma do this without her. The woman standing before her had done more for Layla in the few years she'd known her than some of her own family members.

When she'd met Martha, the older woman took one look at her and told her to "sit her butt down and stay a while." From that moment on, the two women had bonded. Martha had taught Layla how to make gravy, showed her how to plant tomatoes, and held her when her own mother died from breast cancer. Martha definitely had a stake in this.

"Come on," Martha said. "We have to do this, baby."

"I know. Let's go." The night breeze whipped across Layla's cheek. It was way past her bedtime, especially on a school night. Her students would definitely call her on it if she didn't give them her all tomorrow. Peering down at her stomach, she couldn't help the small smile that always accompanied a kick. Being pregnant was a blessing, being a mother was everything to her. "It's going to be okay, son. Mama's going to always take care of you."

They hurried to the door, Layla following close behind Martha. As they approached the green door of the town-house, she once again wondered what she would actually find on the other side. After all, they were getting ready to enter a known, and very active, drug house. Would her heart be able to take it?

Music blared inside the small home, and Layla could hear the muffled sound of voices, laughter. According to the woman who'd called her, the party had been in full swing for hours, with people coming in and out. The smell of smoke seeped through the open window to the side.

Martha nudged Layla with her elbow. "Ready?"

Layla set the bat down for a minute to wipe her sweaty palms, then lifted it up high. "When you are."

The glint of silver in Martha's hand caught Layla's eye. Her mother-in-law never went anywhere without her "piece." The small .38 special stayed in her purse or under her mattress. Layla watched as Martha checked the barrel once more. Then, without another word, Martha kicked in the door.

It was chaos as women screamed and people pushed past her and out the door. Layla's trembling hands held on to the bat for dear life, all while trying to stay upright.

"Where is my son?" Martha demanded, to no one in particular.

Layla scanned the immediate area, locking eyes with the remaining people. The room was trashed, cups on the floor, cigarette butts everywhere. And the smell…it was toxic. She felt bile in her throat rise and before she could stop herself, she threw up on the floor. Ma was behind her, rubbing her back and whispering nonsensical words to her. It took several moments to regain her composure, but she finally stood to her full height and shot Ma a glance.

"I'm sorry," Layla whispered. "I'm okay."

Before last year, Layla had been blissfully ignorant to all the telltale signs of drug abuse. She'd never had to deal with anything remotely like it in her childhood. She'd grown up in the church, spent most of her days in the four walls of her family's place of worship. It wasn't until college that she'd been introduced to alcohol, cigarettes, and men. One man, in particular. The man she thought she'd love forever.

"Don't make me repeat myself," Martha growled, snapping Layla out of her thoughts.

A skinny man shuffled toward them and Layla immediately recognized him. Lincoln's best friend, Rod. Layla had never liked him because she instinctively knew he was trouble. He'd always showed up at inappropriate hours, looking worse for the wear. When she'd met him several years ago, he'd been a healthy, stocky man. Now, he looked thin, frail, and haggard.

He eyed her, before turning to Martha. "He's in the back." He pointed toward a door. "But you shouldn't go back there."

Rod was talking to her now, not Martha. Layla's chin trembled. "Why?"

"You don't want to go back there," he said, a solemn look in his eyes.

Martha grumbled a curse, and waived her gun toward

him. "Rod, get the hell out of here before I tell your wife where you been."

When Rod scurried out of the door, Layla told Martha, "I'll go."

"You sure?"

"Yes."

Layla walked to the closed door, stepping over broken glass and scattered pieces of foil. Sighing, she pushed it open. Passed on out the floor, in a pool of vomit, was her husband.

"Oh no." She dropped her bat and hurried over to him, kneeling down before him. "Lincoln?" She turned him over and shook him. "Get up."

There was no movement, no sign of life. She picked up his wrist and placed two fingers between the bone and the tendon over his radial artery, like she'd been taught to do in the required first aid certification class she'd taken every year since she'd become a teacher. When she finally felt his pulse, she slumped over as relief coursed through her.

She slapped both of his cheeks, and shook him again. "Linc, wake up. Come on, baby. Get up. Please."

Layla startled when she heard movement in the corner of the room. "Who's there?" She'd been so focused on Linc, she hadn't stopped to see if anyone was in the room with him. "Come out, whoever you are."

A man, dressed in a dirty, wrinkled suit crawled out from behind the long, heavy curtains. Layla eyed her discarded bat near the door and considered going for it, but the man didn't seem to know where he was. He had a dazed look in his eyes and a shaky gait as his stood to his feet and walked toward her. She hugged Linc to her and met the man's gaze.

"What do you want?" she asked.

The man's eyes softened. "You should go home. He's

ELLE WRIGHT

hopeless. Just like I am." Without another word, the man shuffled out of the room.

Layla peered down at Linc. She traced the lines of his forehead and the arch of his nose. "Please, Linc. Wake up." She hit him again, and shook him one last time. "Damn-it, wake up!"

Finally, his eyes cracked open. "LaLa," he breathed. "You're here."

His nickname for her, LaLa, used to make her feel so special, so loved. Today, though, it gutted her. "I'm here. Come on, get up."

It took an hour to get him out of the house and settled at Ma's home. She'd bathed him and tucked him in before leaving the spare bedroom.

Martha held out a mug of hot tea when Layla walked into the kitchen, but she declined the offering. "No, thanks, Ma. I'd better go."

"Baby, don't do this. He can get better. We can make sure he does."

The tears that had threatened to fall all night finally fell. Shaking her head, she said, "I can't. I have to do what's best for my kids. You know that."

Martha dabbed her own eyes with a paper towel. "I do." She hugged Layla. "I love you, baby."

Layla rested her chin on Martha's shoulder. "I love you, too, Ma. And I love him, as well. But I can't do this anymore."

Martha pulled back and brushed her hand over Layla's cheek. "I understand. You go home, now. Rest. I'll check in on you in the morning."

Layla nodded. "Thanks."

Slowly, Layla made her way to the door. It took everything in her not to go back, to climb in the bed with Lincoln. But she'd made up her mind. It was over.

120

Turning back to Martha, Layla said, "And please——"

"Layla, I'll keep him away. For now. Until he's better."

"It's for the best," Layla said. "I don't want my kids to be around him when he's like this."

Then, Layla walked out of the house, away from him, and away from their life.

Excerpt: The Closing Bid
DISTINGUISHED GENTLEMEN SERIES

*T*he cold didn't reach his bones. It never did out there. The smell of peanuts and grass, the sound of wood cracking against leather, the roar of the crowd, the feel of the dirt underneath him... it all felt like home to him. The field was his safe place, one of only a handful of safe places in his life.

Christian Knight had spent years building a career as a professional baseball player for the Detroit Jaguars. He was bigger than life there, an integral piece to an important puzzle, and one of the best "closers" in the league. And in a few weeks, he would be stepping on the mound for opening day one last time. The upcoming season would be his final one.

Life for him hadn't been all that easy lately, starting with the discovery of his ex-wife having an affair without regard for his feelings. Having a marriage deteriorate in the public eye should have been the worst thing that he'd ever experience. Finding out about the affair in the pages of a magazine could have stolen that honor. But, no, it was the sudden death of his mother that had Christian questioning everything about his life.

He turned, surveying the empty ballpark. In half an hour, he'd announce his retirement to the world. The decision to end his career so soon had thrown the team into a lurch, but he couldn't imagine staying another year. Because he wasn't the same person who'd vowed to play until he couldn't walk anymore. Baseball didn't define him anymore.

Christian heard the sound of footsteps on grass nearing him and turned. His entertainment attorney, Zara Reid, approached him, a smile on her face. Everything about her commanded respect, from her sensible but sexy suit to her "power pumps" as she called her heels. As always, she looked ready to wheel and deal in a black pencil skirt, silk blouse, and lightweight jacket. Her long hair was pulled back into a neat ponytail and she wore little to no makeup on her smooth brown skin.

He'd been with Zara for five years, and she'd done more for him in that time than his first two agents. Endorsements were rolling in, with everyone from fashion designers to shoe companies to fast-food chains. When he'd signed with her, she'd told him that she worked for him, and assured him that she would fight hard for him. So far, she'd never let him down, proving herself as his strongest advocate time and time again.

"Are you ready?"

He sighed and stuffed his hands into the pockets of his dress pants. If it were up to him, he would have worn jeans and a t-shirt. But Zara had suggested he look a little more "put together". He chuckled when Zara muttered a curse about dirt on her Manolo Blahniks.

"Shit, it's cold as hell out here."

"It's March. In Michigan." He shook his head at her

outfit. "Maybe next time wear a coat?" He paused. "I don't want to take a lot of questions," he said. "Two, maybe three."

Zara sighed. "How about five? This is a big deal. You're not only retiring, but your announcing your new mentorship program. We want to make sure your fans know you're not going away completely."

Christian held up one hand, indicating five questions were okay.

"Two things—this press conference is going to blow my phone up with requests for interviews. It will also open you up to questions about non-baseball things. And I need you to keep your cool."

He glared at his agent. "I always keep my cool."

Zara sighed heavily. "Under normal circumstances." She squeezed his arm. "Christian, you've had so much to deal with in the last year. Your emotions are raw. Don't assume they won't bring up Meena."

Hearing his ex-wife's name only served to heighten his emotions. The melancholy he'd felt when the plane landed earlier that morning at the Detroit Metropolitan Airport ebbed a little when he'd stepped out on the field, but now… The last thing he wanted was a rehash of the hell he'd been through over the past several months.

Christian hated the press, had rarely granted interviews because he valued his privacy. He didn't post on Facebook, he rarely tweeted, didn't even know how to SnapChat, and didn't take selfies or pictures of his food to post on Instagram. When he granted interviews, there was always a bigger purpose—new contract negotiations, community support for much needed programs, or after-game impressions. That's it. Even then, he didn't like the questions, the lights, the intrusion into his private life.

He'd tried his best to stay out of the tabloids during his

career. He had a reputation for being a stand-up man—someone who honored his commitments, someone who gave back to his community for all the right reasons, and someone who didn't do things for "likes" or "retweets". All of that changed last summer, during the height of the season. But it wasn't because of anything he'd done. It was all on Meena—and the journalist who'd exposed the prostitution ring his wife had been involved in. Which, in turn, revealed the torrid affair she'd been having with the General Manager of one of his rival teams.

"Christian?" Zara peered up at him, concern in her brown eyes. "I just it's best to be prepared for the worst."

"I'm fine. *If* they bring up Meena, I'll politely deflect."

His agent shot him a disbelieving look, then waved a hand of dismissal in his direction. "Fine. About the interviews... it's your ball game. Pun intended. You tell me how many you want to do."

The answer to that was easy. Zero. But he knew going into this that was impossible. So, he threw out the next best number. "One."

Her eyes widened. "One? What the hell? Christian, give me something to work with. I'm trying to set you up for your after-baseball money. I can't do that if you continue to play coy with reporters."

Shrugging, he said, "We've already had this discussion multiple times since I told you I was done with the game. Aside from a few endorsements, I'm okay not doing commentary or staying involved in the politics of the league. Hence, the reason why I'm retiring."

Zara rolled her eyes. Hard. "Fine. I'm going to have to fire you."

Christian laughed. "Fire me? Isn't that backwards. You work for me, so technically, wouldn't I have to let you go?"

"Whatever. I only get paid when I work. Which means, I need to wheel and deal for you."

He shook his head, still chuckling at his friend. "Do you threaten to fire all of your clients? Or just me?"

"Just you. You're the only one I call friend." Zara cleared her throat.

They'd discussed her role in his career once he actually retired and had both agreed that she would continue to do what he needed her to do, whether it was a lot or a little. But she had earned a permanent spot on his life's journey because she'd been a good friend to him. That would never change. "We'll talk about this later. You good?"

Nodding, he said, "Yes. Let's go."

The warmth that had blazed in her eyes less than a minute ago was replaced by a steely resolve that often indicated that Zara was ready for battle. She tugged on her suit jacket and smoothed the hair on her head. "I'll be there the entire time. Stick to the talking points, keep your responses simple."

Without another word, Zara turned on her heels and stalked off the field, muttering curses along the way about dirt, expensive shoes and cold Michigan weather.

Christian followed after her at a distance, taking in the scenery around him. The unusually warm March day was one for the record books. The Detroit skyline served as the backdrop, with the Renaissance Tower standing tall under clear, blue skies. Christian couldn't imagine living anywhere else.

His mother moved around a lot, having worked as a traveling nurse. Christian had lived in Chicago, Fort Lauderdale, Phoenix, Sacramento, and Tuscaloosa, Alabama all before he turned fifteen. When his mother took a job at St. Joseph Mercy Hospital in Ypsilanti, Michigan, he'd balked at the notion of leaving the warmer climate, another school, and his team at the time. But he'd fallen in love with the change of seasons, and later, with the state. It was destiny when he'd been drafted by the Detroit Jaguars, one of two professional baseball teams in the city. Although, he could technically go anywhere since he would no longer be bound by a contract, he planned to stay in the Detroit area.

Thinking of his mother, of the sacrifices she'd made to ensure he'd always had what he needed to thrive, put a damper in his mood. Because he missed her. She should be standing beside him when he made this announcement. She should be helping him run his mentoring program. She should be there. Period. The fact that she wasn't made his chest ache and his eyes burn with unshed tears. There would be time for emotion later, though. He couldn't give in to the sadness. Not now.

Christian brushed off his suit and straightened his cuffs as he stepped into the building. Turning, he spotted the bay of elevators ahead, leading to the offices and the player locker room. The press conference would take place there. *Zara's idea.*

Speaking of… *Where the hell is she?* He scanned the area. Few people milled around, maintenance workers readying the ballpark for opening day in a few weeks, cameramen hauling heavy equipment, team staff carrying out daily business. But no Zara.

Frowning, he checked the time. Maybe she went ahead to make sure everything was set up. He pushed the "up" button for the elevator. When the car arrived, he stepped on. Seconds later, he exited, stopping in his tracks at the sight of Meena standing there like she owned the place.

He drew in a slow, steady breath to calm his anger. They hadn't seen each other since the divorce proceedings, which was fine with him. His ex-wife had deliberately prolonged the process, instructing her attorneys to file motion after motion about everything, despite the existence of an ironclad prenuptial agreement. What should have taken sixty days had taken twelve months. During the settlement conference, security had to be called because Meena had threatened his attorney. Luckily for him, he'd hired one of the best attorneys in Southeast Michigan, a woman known as The Divorce Whisperer. When she was done with Meena and her attorney, he'd walked out a happy man.

"Christian?" Meena smiled, smoothing a hand over her long weave.

His gaze dropped to her attire. The sheer, skin tight dress she wore left little to the imagination, exposing swaths of her brown skin. They'd met at the now-closed Hard Rock Café Detroit during her lunch hour. He'd met Zara for lunch, and she'd come to the restaurant with her co-workers. Meena used to work for General Motors as a Financial Analyst. When they'd met five years ago, she was sweet, humble, and beautiful. And he'd fallen in love with her for all those reasons, and because she was nothing like the women who threw themselves at him after every game. But the woman standing in front of him now was nothing like the seemingly innocent woman to whom he'd proposed.

Over the two years, she'd transformed into another woman right before his eyes. Still gorgeous, but she'd developed an air of superiority that drove him insane. And her attitude? Nice-nasty and just plain rude. This Meena spent time staging her Instagram pics, shopping at exclusive shops and purchasing expensive brands. This Meena cared little about the people he was so passionate about.

"What are you doing here?" he asked.

"I needed to see you."

"For what? We don't have anything to talk about."

Meena straightened her shoulders. "I think we do." She stepped forward. "Christian, I hate how things ended with us. I didn't mean to hurt you."

Christian chose to remain silent. He'd been in this position before, faced with a remorseful Meena. Soon, the tears would fall. And when he rebuffed her yet again, the claws would come out.

"I just think we should clear the air. I've been thinking about you. I'm so sorry about your mom. I know how much she meant to you."

He folded his arms over his chest and narrowed his gaze on her. The passage of time hadn't dissipated the resentment he felt toward his ex. The heat of anger flushed through his body as she stood there, staring at him, waiting for him to make her feel better about her sorry attempt at "heartfelt" condolences. Because he knew better. He knew that Meena never cared for his mother. And he knew that because she'd admitted in court that she couldn't stand her.

The two had never really gotten along, but the already strained relationship between his mother and his ex-wife had been destroyed during the divorce trial. Rosalind Knight had never been one to hold her tongue, and Meena had gotten many an earful after the scandal broke.

She shifted on her feet. "When I heard she passed, I wanted to call you."

But you didn't.

"I tried to come to the funeral."

"Is there a point to this conversation? What do you want?" Christian could not stand there and listen to her pretend to care that his mother died. Meena wanted something from him and he would not spend another minute or even a dime over the court-ordered spousal support on her.

"I can't give my condolences to you? She was my mother—?"

"Don't," he warned.

"Christian, you—"

"This is a restricted area. How did you even get in here?"

She held up her All-Access pass, the one he'd given her last season when he'd made an effort to try to save their marriage. Before all hell broke loose.

Christian spotted a security guard to his left and walked over to him. "What's up, Ron?"

Ron Porter grinned. "Welcome back, Christian. The wife wanted me to tell you that she's sorry for your loss."

"Thanks. Tell Elaine I appreciate the flowers she sent. It meant a lot to me."

"I certainly will."

Leaning forward, Christian said, "See that woman over there?"

Ron looked over Christian's shoulder and his eyes widened. "You mean… that's your—"

Christian clasped the older man's shoulder. "Yes. That's her. Can you escort her out of the building? And make sure her access pass is destroyed because she is no longer Mrs. Knight."

"Sure, Christian. I'll get right on that."

Ron approached Meena and asked her to leave. As his ex-wife tried to cause a scene, screaming his name over and over again while threatening Ron with legal action if he touched her, Christian walked away.

About the Author

There was never a time when Elle Wright wasn't about to start a book, wasn't already deep in a book—or had just finished one. She grew up believing in the importance of reading, and became a lover of all things romance when her mother gave her her first romance novel. She lives in Michigan.

Join the Elle Wright Reader Group!

Connect with Elle!
www.ellewright.com
info@ellewright.com

Also by Elle Wright

Edge of Scandal Series

The Forbidden Man

His All Night

Her Kind of Man

All He Wants for Christmas

Once Upon a Bridesmaid Series

Beyond Forever

Jacksons of Ann Arbor

It's Always Been You

Wherever You Are

Because Of You

All For You

Wellspring Series

Touched By You

Enticed By You

Pleasured By You

DECADES: A Journey of African American Romance

Made To Hold You (The 80s)

Distinguished Gentlemen Series

The Closing Bid

Made in the USA
Monee, IL
26 May 2021

69504803R00090